ALSO BY CRAIG A. ROBERTSON

BOOKS IN THE RYANVERSE:

THE FOREVER SERIES (2016)

THE FOREVER LIFE, BOOK 1
THE FOREVER ENEMY, BOOK 2
THE FOREVER FIGHT, BOOK 3
THE FOREVER QUEST, BOOK 4
THE FOREVER ALLIANCE, BOOK 5
THE FOREVER PEACE, BOOK 6

THE GALAXY ON FIRE SERIES (2017)

EMBERS, BOOK 1
FLAMES, BOOK 2
FIRESTORM, BOOK 3
FIRES OF HELL, BOOK 4
DRAGON FIRE, BOOK 5
ASHES, BOOK 6

RISE OF ANCIENT GODS SERIES (2018)

RETURN OF THE ANCIENT GODS, **BOOK 1**
RAGE OF THE ANCIENT GODS, **BOOK 2**
TORMENT OF THE ANCIENT GODS, **BOOK 3**
WRATH OF THE ANCIENT GODS, Book 4 (Due in early 2019)

STAND-ALONE NOVELS

THE CORPORATE VIRUS (2016)
TIME DIVING (2013)
THE INNERgLOW EFFECT (2010)
WRITE NOW! The Prisoner of NaNoWriMo (2009)
ANON TIME (2009)

DRAGON FIRE

BOOK FIVE OF THE *GALAXY ON FIRE SERIES*

by Craig Robertson

Never Stop Believing in Magic!

Imagine-It Publishing
El Dorado Hills, CA

ISBN: 978-0-9997742-0-5 (Print)
978-0-9989253-9-4 (E-Book)

Cover design by Jessica Bell

Editing and Formatting services by Polgarus Studio
Available at http://www.polgarusstudio.com

Editorial Assistance By Michael R. Blanche

First Edition 2018
Second Edition 2019

Imagine-It Publishing

This book is dedicated to the innocent mass-shooting victims, especially the children, as well as their families, and their communities. We face such horrors much too often. They all deserve *better*.

Note: Glossary of Terms Is Located at the End of the Book

ONE

"I say we may safely ignore both you *and* your report." Harsher words had never been spoken in the chamber of the Secure Council. But High Wedge Lesset was a person of passion and excessive pride. Plus, he wielded the ultimate power both on the council and in the empire. His word became dogma.

Transit High Wedge Varsor was aware of the position he'd just been placed in. He never liked the council Prime, but he'd never openly tangled with him, either. Most who had were soon dead. The few who survived did so in anonymity, serving in some far-flung backwash of the empire. Still, his intelligence report was both accurate and alarming. To the best of his knowledge, nothing like this had ever confronted the mighty armies of the Adamant. He only hoped that doing the right thing didn't get him and his family deleted.

"I will overlook the tone of your remarks," said Varsor evenly, "in the interest of the security of the empire. I cannot, however, turn a blind eye to your flippant disregard of a potentially critical development."

The other ten members of the council either sat stone-like or looked away. The certainty of a cataclysmic collision was not something any of them wanted to witness. It wasn't that any of them were kindly, empathetic, or actually interested. It was that the impending bloodshed would only cause confusion and delay in the business of the council. Nothing useful would come of it. By tradition, the combatant who survived would choose the loser's

1

successor. For the other ten, there wasn't even the prospect of juicy political infighting when the confrontation was complete.

"Do you have so many mites in your ears that you failed to comprehend? As council Prime it is my duty to the emperor to keep these proceedings focused and moving along at a productive pace. The airing of inconsequential, irrelevant, and imbecilic issues runs contrary to those efforts. Please defer for the remainder of your designated-speaking time, or I will be forced to remove it by fiat."

"I will *not* defer my time when I have a report that needs to be addressed. My spies have constructed a cohesive picture of alien planets actively working together ahead of our invasion of their sector. This is unheard of and must factor into our planning."

Leaning forward, Lesset angrily knuckled the table. "I will address your precious concerns, fool. If every world in the sector lashed their planets together like a gigantic raft and swung their pitiful paddles at our forces, it would alter *nothing*. We always sweep away resistance in one fell swoop. If these primitives fight separately, together, or not at all, they will die as civilizations just as swiftly and completely. The only possible difference it will make is how harshly we deal with them when the fighting stops. Are you as happy as a pup sucking on his mate's *teat* now, Varsor? May we proceed?"

"I would like to query the other council members to see if they feel this new and unprecedented cooperation should be factored into our assault plans," Varsor said defiantly.

Lesset glowered at the toad he was facing. Then he spoke loudly with a melodramatic tone. "Fine. I call for a vote. All in favor of listening to the squeals of this frightened lunatic, signal so by raising his paw. I see no paws raised," he said without even pausing to take a breath, "so the motion fails just like its author. High Wing Oltimure, I believe the floor is now yours for the next ten minutes."

"What of my remaining time?" howled Varsor as he leapt to his feet.

"By fiat, I declare you are out of time," replied Lesset coolly. He drew his sidearm and blew away most of Varsor's throat.

Varsor seized his throat and tried to keep his head from toppling. Blood geysered through his digits. He took a step toward Lesset.

"No, not in this direction," screamed Lesset. "You'll ... ah, there you've done it. You have ruined my *favorite* jacket. I have half a mind to call a medic to resuscitate you, just so I may kill you again for that affront."

Well before Lesset finished, Varsor was dead on the floor.

"Everything that fellow did was annoying. Look at the mess he's made," remarked Lesset casually. "Well, there's nothing for it, we'll have to continue the meeting covered in a traitor's blood. No time to clean up and remain on schedule." He pointed to Oltimure. "Sorry, you're down to six minutes now. Please begin."

"I defer my allotted time, Prime." Oltimure wished to remain as invisible as possible while Lesset's blood lust ran so high. He was a wise and prudent High Wing. He was a survivor.

TWO

"Jon, swim over to me. I see a turtle under the pontoon," Jenna yelled to me joyously.

She was always full of joy, come to think of it. She exuded the stuff. She was my best friend, even though I only saw her for two weeks once a year. That's when both our families vacationed together in the log-cabin campground near town. For us, it was Tom Sawyer and Nancy Drew all rolled into one nonstop adventure. She was ten; I was about to turn nine.

The specific problem I faced was that I didn't want to swim over to where she was on the floating platform. It hadn't been a full hour since I had that ice cream cone. I didn't want to risk drowning because of a stomach cramp. My parents swore it was a certainty and made me promise years before never to attempt it. My dad said it was because we were such a poor family that if I died, they couldn't afford to bury me. Mom slugged him good for that crack, but he just laughed. Dad was always funny, a regular cutup.

"I'll be there in a few minutes," I shouted back as I checked my Timex.

"No, he'll be gone by then." She pouted. From two hundred yards I could see it plain as day.

I decided if I swam real slow, maybe my stomach wouldn't know I was cheating the clock, and I wouldn't go under in pain. I always told everybody I wanted to be an astronaut. Heck fire, they took all kinds of risks. I had to stop being a sissy and get used to it. I walked out in the lake as far as I could and then dog-paddled slower than any dog ever did all the way to the float. I looked back at the shore. I was not, in fact, dead. Maybe my parents were wrong. Maybe there were exceptions to the rule. Or maybe the rules didn't apply to me. That thought made me kind of happy.

"Over here, Jonny. He's nearly gone."

I walked over to where Jenna had her torso craned down to view the underside of the platform.

"How do you know it's a boy?" I asked as I bent over to join her.

"It's leaving before I'm done looking at it. Only a boy would be so rude."

"Oh, ya mean like this?" I ripped a juicy fart.

"Oh, you're so gross. Now look," she pointed, "you can just see him over there."

Sure enough, there was a snapper turtle pulling at some plants growing on a pontoon.

"You know why he's diving down?" I asked very seriously.

"No. Did we scare him?"

"Naw. He saw us, sure. But he's going under to be able to bite off one of our toes when we get back in the water."

"He's not that smart, Jonny. You're just trying to scare me."

"No, it's true. It's all instinct with them. He knows we have to try to make it back to shore sooner or later. Even if we wait for it to get dark, he'll be happier because he'll be more invisible. Why, last year over at Lake Dakota, a kid got—"

I was about to cook up some bull about his bones being picked clean like a piranha ate him, but Jenna was up and running. She dived into the water so fast she was a blur.

She surfaced, threw her hair off her face, and challenged me, "Come on, scaredy pants. See if you can beat me to the shore." With that, she spun and started swimming like a pro.

I flew into the water and swam for all I was worth. Just when I was about to catch her, maybe ten yards from the beach, a thought hit me. I started treading water. She scurried up onto the muddy sand and turned to me with her hands triumphantly planted on her hips.

"Hey, Mr. Slow Boat to China, I knew you—"

Jenna stopped talking when I lifted my feet off the bottom and screamed in terror. I disappeared under the water for as long as I could hold my breath, then jumped up real high. Reaching for my feet, I screamed, "He's got me." Then I went under briefly. The next time I was at the surface, I yelled, "Find a gun and shoot him!" Then I vanished under the water.

By the time I was forced to come up for air, Jenna was by my side. She kicked and splashed with her arms like a girl possessed. Then she put her arm across my neck, the way we were taught when saving a drowning person. She began to walk/swim, dragging me to safety.

I wasn't sure what to do, but when we got to shore, and she saw I wasn't bleeding, she gave me a stern look. Then she began to laugh. We plopped onto a beach towel and both had a good laugh. Jenna was the best.

"Jon, when you die, would you rather be alone or with somebody?" she asked me after we calmed down.

"What a weirdo question," I replied. "How should I know? I mean, it's not like they always give you a choice, you know?"

She pulled her knees up tightly to her chest. "I died alone, and I didn't like it one bit. I was scared *and* lonely. You should die with people you love all around you." She sounded quiet, authoritative on the topic.

"One prob, goofball. You're talking to me, so you're not *dead*. That means you never died, because if you did, you'd be dead."

"Can't you be serious for one minute of your life, Jon Ryan?"

"What?" I reached over and pinched her hard.

She jumped. "Ouch. Why'd you do that?"

"To prove you're alive. I rest my case."

"Well, Perry Mason, you miss my point. I died alone." She pointed at the pontoon. "I was swimming to that very float, and I bumped my head on it and drowned. I was all alone. You didn't come up here in time, or you'd have been with me and I wouldn't have died." She reached over and punched me. "It was all *your* fault." Then she threw herself belly down on the blanket. "But I forgive you because I love you."

What? Did a girl just say she *loved* me? Did I need to marry her now? Gross.

"How can what never happened be my fault when I wasn't here?"

"Exactly. Now remember, you should die in the company of loved ones. Okay?"

"Sure. I promise. Hey, maybe you can be there when I croak. That way I'll have all the company I need."

She sat and balled up, clutching her legs tightly again. "No, Jonathan, I can't be there. You won't die for several billion years. By then, I'll probably be too busy somewhere else. Who knows, maybe I'll have kids of my own and can't leave them because they'll need me."

"What, you gonna have a family after you're dead and gone?"

She looked at me like my fourth grade teacher Mrs. Blum. I was so scared of that witch. "I may be dead, but who says I'll be gone?"

"Can we like talk about something less creepy?"

"Sure. How about a snack?"

"I'm always up for that."

"My mom packed us some sandwiches," she pointed, "over there. Grab the basket."

I retrieved it and she studied the contents.

"Jon, I will miss you so terribly much, you know, after I die and you won't, for almost ever."

What a screwy conversation. "I'll miss you, too." I said more as a question.

"No, you won't. You'll have long forgotten me. Plus, you'll be busy saving everybody and trying not to get yourself killed. No, by the time you die, no one will remember me at all. I'll be just some silly girl who bumped her head."

"Please stop saying that. You're scaring me."

She rested an ice-cold hand on my forearm. "I know you're scared, Jonny. But don't be. You're not going to die now, not today." She angled her head. "Who knows, maybe you never will. Or maybe it'll be tomorrow. But you will not die at your own hand today."

"Please, Jenna, you're freaking me out. What? Are you saying I'll commit suicide? Jenna, please help me."

"Jonathan, I am." She leaned over and kissed me gently on the forehead. Her lips were as cold as deep space. "Now you go show that mean robot who's boss."

"Where will you be? What mean robot?"

She extended her arms. "Right here at our lake. I'll always be here. Now go, before I start missing you even more."

I'd looked toward the lake when she gestured to it. When I looked back, Jenna was gone. *Poof.* She'd simply disappeared. It was like she was never there but like she was always there, at our lake. I started to cry but forgot to. I was distracted by something. Something painful. Something bad. Something slapping my face in rage and hate.

My eyes popped open. I gasped. I tried to sit up. I was lashed down and couldn't move an inch. Someone slapped my cheek again, very hard.

"Wake up you piece of rat *shit*," wailed EJ as he drew his arm above his head to repeat the action. "I don't have time to waste getting a useless machine out of his trance." He pounded my face again.

"Stop!" screamed a female voice from somewhere. "He's coming to. Stop hitting him." It took a second, but I figured it out. It was Sapale, my Sapale, not the little girl I'd saved.

EJ lowered his arm and peered at me from directly above. "Why, so he is." Then he slapped me twice more. "Now I'm done; for now, that is."

"Leave him be, you monster!" Sapale yelled.

He turned to her. There she was, cowering in the corner of the large room. "STFU, bitch. Remember my warning. If you so much as help him take a *piss*, I'll kill your entire family, kids first."

Wow, he was crazy mad. And I hadn't urinated since the day I became an android. What kind of stupid threat was that?

Sapale shrank farther into the corner. It was pitiful to watch.

"Now, as for you, Sleeping Beauty, here's the deal. I need Risrav and I need it *now*."

"Huh?" was all I could muster. Some of my components were still not back online yet.

"Risrav! You know, lunkhead, the stone that negates mine, stops me from using my magic on you?" He slapped me again.

"I'm awake now, if you hadn't noticed," I snarked.

"I know but beating the crap out of you is better than sex."

"Now I know we're not identical. You're an *idiot*."

Yeah, he slapped me a few more times, but it was worth it.

"Now, I need that rock. I went over you good, but I can't find it. I have two options. One, you can tell me where it is, then I kill you quickly and painlessly."

"Don't even tell me choice two. That one sounds delectable."

"Smart ass. Option two is I rip you apart piece by tiny piece."

"I said don't tell me number two. Now I can't decide which is better."

"But if I do that I risk damaging Risrav. *That* I can't afford to do. So, cupcake of shit, which will it be? Oh, and just as an added incentive, if you just tell me where it is, I promise not to kill Sapale before your weeping eyes. If you force me to grind you up, she gets the same treatment."

I ran some quick systems checks. Everything was on and functional. My entire body was strapped to a metal table with redundancy. I couldn't see my hands, but they were balled into fists and covered with a hard shell, maybe a cast. EJ was taking no chances. Well, he was taking too great a risk by waking me up at all. I was going to get out of this and spring my plan on him with extreme prejudice, the sorry son of a bitch. By the way, I'd hidden Risrav in my scrotum. Yeah, clever of me, eh? I knew that if this exact scenario ever transpired, EJ would never check there.

"I'll make you a deal," I said coolly. "Let the both of us go, and I'll give you the rune."

He rolled his eyes and shook his head. "Let me think about it. No. That's would be the dumbest thing for me to do. No, pal, the only way you're leaving this room is as scrap."

"I'll sweeten the deal. Seriously, listen hard. If you let us go, I won't do to you what I was planning to."

"It might help if you told me what I'm being *spared*, lame brain."

"*Spoiler* alert. You'll just have to trust me."

"Let me repeat that last line back to you. *You'll just have to trust me.* Do you think in your tiny processors that there is the remotest chance in hell I'd trust you to do *anything*? You must have skipped your last hundred upgrades, moron."

"Oh well, don't say I didn't warn you."

He folded his arms. "You know what, Jon? I'm sick as shit of hearing this brave-gonna-get-out-of-this crap. Hell, I've said the same things myself, back in the day. But, seriously, you're not going to manage a last-minute miracle. You're not going to save the damsel in distress," he pointed to Sapale. "Most poignantly, you're not going to see tomorrow, so spare me the macho speech."

"J ... Jenna told me I wasn't going to die today. Maybe tomorrow, she said, but definitely not today."

"Who the hell's *Jenna*. I need to find her and let her know her prediction was the opposite of correct."

"She's at the lake, our lake."

"Oh great, I must have fried your brain. You're delusional. Crap, now I can't be certain you'll appreciate the fact that I'm killing you when I do." He turned and paced away. The dude was seriously pissed. My, how I'd changed. I was criminally insane *and* a whack job.

"Jon, I'm so sorry," said Sapale, taking advantage of EJ's silence. "At least we'll be together again in death."

God, I loved that woman. "Let's not get ahead of ourselves here. We're getting out of this." I nodded my head at EJ. "He's the one who should be worried."

"I said no stupid bravado," he snarled, and he slapped me again. "You're making me nauseous."

"Well, chalk one up for Good Jon," I replied with a stupid grin.

He leaned over and came nose to nose with me. "Oh, so you're the *good* me, and I'm the *evil* me. That how you see it, chump?"

"To be fair, many people agree with me, EJ."

"You're such a fool, such a Pollyanna. You still think it's about good versus evil, right versus wrong." He harrumphed. "What a piece of work."

"So, Master Yoda, what is it about if it isn't what it's always been about?"

He thumbed his chest angrily. "It's all about me. Whatever *I* want, whatever *I* need, and whatever *I* fancy. Period. End of story. Do Not Pass Go, and Do *Not* Collect Two Hundred Dollars."

"I'm so glad I'm not you. You're more pathetic than I ever imagined.

Seriously, EJ, do yourself a favor and blow your head off. If you're too chicken, I volunteer to help."

"Enough with the wasting of my endless time. Back to the issue at hand. What'll it be? The easy way or the hard way? You've got thirty seconds."

Captain, are you there? Sir, we'd lost you, but I detect your signal. Captain, what is your status? Al popped into my head. Oh yeah, I'd been gone a while, hadn't I? Wait, he had to know about the electrical discharge and my seeing EJ. Until my systems went down, he had access to everything I saw.

I'm here. My status is debatable. My body is functioning well. EJ, however, has me tied up and is about to begin removing parts. Oh, Sapale's here and says hi.

We regret to learn about your situation, sir. May we help in any way, General Ryan?

What was with all the formality?

I don't think so. Wish you could.

I guess that softens the blow of our update, sir. There are approximately ten thousand Adamant troops swarming up the hill to your location. As we speak, the skies are filling with warships. We estimate they will overrun your position in the next four to five minutes.

It was then I noted the very odd look on EJ's face, sort of puzzled mixed with baffled. He could hear Al, too. Of course, he could. He's done it all the time on our shared voyage with Al on *Ark 1*. Al had to know that fact. Wait, wait. That's why he was speaking so formally. He knew I'd be suspicious, but EJ almost certainly wouldn't. Hell, it'd been two *billion* years since they last spoke.

Then either way I'm a goner, Al. Tell Blessing *I love her and that I'll miss you both dearly.* I was stretching things out. Calling *Stingray* by her real name would let Al know I read him clearly. If EJ bought the ruse, he'd want to eavesdrop a while, but he also had to split soon if he wanted to avoid capture. It'd take him a couple minutes to get me off this table, so the likelihood of him taking me with him was dropping to no way.

Remember the Zeno-One Protocol, Al? After I'm dead, you must execute it at once. Do you copy?

Not the dreaded Zeno-One Protocol, Captain. I do not know if I will be able to perform it, it being so dreaded.

Al, listen carefully. I'm no good at being noble, but it doesn't take much to see that the problems of three little artificial life-forms don't amount to a hill of beans in this crazy world. Someday you'll understand that. You must execute the protocol. The part where you must mix the hyperdrive fuel with the neutron stream will be tricky, pal, but I know you can do it. I know you're stronger than you know.

God that sounded awful. Way too corny, but I was ad-libbing to beat the band. It must've been working, because EJ was still angling his head and staring at the floor. Now, if he didn't kill me gratuitously, I might not die today. I had to guess he'd leave me alive, so he could someday recover Risrav. If he killed me here and now, the Adamant would gain possession of my remains, and he'd never get the rune. Then again, he was insane, so it was hard to count on anything.

General Jonathan Ryan, it has been an honor and a privilege to serve alongside you. I will faithfully initiate the Zeno-One Protocol upon confirmation of your demise. God speed, my captain.

"Okay, I'll bite. What the hell is the Zeno-One Protocol?" demanded EJ.

I did my best to look shocked. "How did you kn ... Wait, you can still *hear* Al, can't you, you *scoundrel*?"

"Get over your damn self, pissant. I have to get the hell out of here, but I want to know." He pulled a blaster out of his belt and pointed it at Sapale. "I don't think I have to tell you I'll do it, Ryan."

Holy *crap*! Now I had to come up with some version of the bullshit protocol I invented to stall for more time. If I failed to convince him, he might realize the entire Al call was a con.

"It ... it's nothing that involves you ..."

EJ started a countdown. "Three ... two ..."

"Okay, stop. I'll tell you everything. The Zeno-One Protocol is a suicide procedure designed to incapacitate and possibly destroy the vortex. I can't allow it to fall into enemy hands. There, that's it."

"All that drama about self-destructing one damn ship. Man, I wish I had time to kill you, squirt. I'd be doing you and the universe a big favor. But, I'll have to save that until next time, sucker." He mock saluted me and tipped his imaginary hat to Sapale. Then he ran from the room. His ship had to be close by.

"Thank Davdiad, he left you alive," said Sapale rushing to my side.

"It won't—"

I started to say it wouldn't take him long to discover our lies, but Sapale had her lips pressed to mine so hard I couldn't say a word. I started talking with my mouth shut. That got her to open her eyes and look at me kind of funny. She pulled back a few inches.

"That was great, honey, but Al made all that up. EJ'll be back in a few seconds. Release me as fast as you can."

Fortunately, she must have seen EJ strap me in, because she moved nimbly to free me. It took a full minute. I knew EJ was overdue, even madder than he was to begin with.

"To the vortex," I said heading for the door.

"But your hands," she shouted.

That's when I got a good look at them. They were steel-jacketed. EJ had actually molded steel mittens on me to secure my weapons.

"No time. I left it open. I'll think of something by the ..."

Time was up. A plasma bolt struck the wall between us. EJ was back.

Sapale whipped a pistol from the back of her waist and returned fire. She just missed him, and he jerked back out of sight.

"Come with me," she said. "My family is in the next room. I can't leave them. He'll butcher them."

I couldn't disagree with her, but we were out of time. I nodded, and we ran.

EJ figured out where we were going. He must have sprinted the back-way, because he blasted the door frame just after we shot through it. The three adults and two kids jumped to their feet.

"We need to fight our way to his ship," she said to the frightened group. "Pick up a child and stay behind us."

Sapale shoulder rolled out the door and opened fire in EJ's direction. He tried to get off a round, but she had him pinned back.

"*Go*," she shouted.

I led the family out the door and to the right. Sapale kept up a blistering line of fire on the corner EJ hid behind.

When we were all around the turn, I yelled, "We're clear. Retreat."

She backed away but never stopped blasting. The two walls that made the corner were chewed to bits. She ducked in next to me. She held up a hand signal for *stop*. Then she used the one for *I'm going to look*. Sapale needed to see if EJ was following or had taken another path. Her head wasn't a millimeter past the edge when a blast struck the wall. EJ was a coming. She stuck her gun around the corner and fired blindly while she signaled with her left hand for us to go.

"Two lefts and a right," I said in her ear, indicating where the ship was. Then I led the group away as fast as we could move.

We made it to *Stingray* in no time. I could hear the fierce firefight down the hall coming closer.

"Al," I held up my hands, "We gotta get these off. Otherwise we're sitting ducks."

"Place them on the utility bench," he replied. After I had, he said, "This will take time. I can cut through safely, but if I go too fast, the heat will melt your hands. They're no good to us if they don't work."

"Do your best."

A tiny laser beam started cutting the steel. Sparks flew, and I felt the temperature rise inside the covering.

"Estimated time to completion?" I asked.

"Ten to fifteen minutes, maybe longer."

"Crap, that's too long. Try and hustle."

The hull sounded off with a plasma bolt. They were here.

Sapale vaulted through the door and pressed up against the hatch frame. She fired blindly down the corridor.

"Al says ten minutes for my hand. Can you hold him off that long?"

She shrugged and smiled. Okay, odd thing to do in a tense situation.

"I could try if you'd like. I'd rather do this." She pointed her left hand at the floor and command prerogatives sprung to the deck. The wall instantly sealed. "Vortex manipulator, take us to the remnants of planet Earth," she called out.

I was stunned.

She walked over to me and looked down at the cutting process. "Do you ever get used to that nausea?" she asked casually.

"You feel it, too?" Then I furrowed up my brow. "Of course, you do. Hey, Als, any sign of pursuit?"

"None so far, Form One."

"What the hell's the one for?" I asked with mild irritation.

"It is customary to address the senior Form as *One* and other ones numerically down the line. Sapale is Form *Two* in this case," responded *Stingray*.

"Oh," I mumbled. "Makes sense, I guess."

"We're so pleased you condone SOP, Pilot," responded Al.

"Can it and keep cutting, Al." To Sapale, I remarked, "So Toño gave you the Deavoriath tools, too." I bobbed my head. "Seems reasonable."

"Even though I didn't have a vortex, he figured they were useful anyway. Remember, he was putting them in a lot of people for a while there."

Yeah, during the fight with the Last Nightmare, he equipped all the Project Ark astronauts and a lot of human pilots with command prerogatives. That way we could field as many vortices as possible for the fight.

"I, for one, am glad he did," I said with a wink. "Why don't you check on your family. I'm good here." I nodded to my hand.

She went to them and everyone joined in a big old group hug. Sweet.

THREE

Sapale sat around the mess table with big mugs of hot coffee. She tucked her family in with a bite to eat and a place to lay down. They were shaken, but they were tough. They'd be okay. Sapale said she wasn't sure where to take them. Kaljax was spiraling down the toilet. I told her about Vorpace and how the humans there would be glad to provide them sanctuary. She said she's consider it.

"So, the kiss thing," I began while studying the tabletop, "I guess it means we're a thing again?"

"By the Sacred Veils you're just a dense as the day I died. Are you really honing that skill, or is it just instinctive?"

I threw my palms up. "What?"

"No, Jon, we're not back together. I told you I *loved* you and the first thing I did when EJ was gone was to plant a wet one on your lips. That's the new way of saying *get lost* in Hirn." She turned a shoulder to me.

Okay, I think that meant *yes*, but it could sort of be interpreted as a *no*. Why didn't she just say what she was feeling? Oh, yeah, she was a woman. Nearly forgot. I would make a command decision and go with the assumption—no, the *certainty* that she loved me and that we were back together again. Yes. That's how I'd play it. No, that's how I would *proceed*.

"I, for one, never stopped loving you," I said honestly. "If I'd known Toño had downloaded you to an android when it happened, I'd have woken myself up from death to find you." That came out well. I swelled internally.

"When you came to me on Kaljax just after you turned back on, I was in a dark and lonely place. I hated EJ so much I couldn't separate you from him. Before you tell me that's a silly notion, please try to understand how horrible life was with him. Two billion years of his increasing cruelty, loss of humanity, and growing insanity was bleak. I was his prisoner, and that gave him great satisfaction. When you turned up at the door, I hated you. Hell, I hated all males." She bundled herself up in her arms.

"But after you left, I worked through it." She turned back to face me. "I remembered how kind and gentle you were. I remembered that you were a *good* man. I remembered how much I loved you."

"Always will. Nothing anybody can do about that."

"And we'll be together forever," she said, smiling.

Oh boy. Better tell her about the Ralph Clause.

"Now here's the funny thing," I began.

She most definitely frowned. "Why don't I like the sound of that? Wait, are you remarried already?"

"No, of course I'm not married." I shrugged. "Haven't been for billions of years. No, it's that there's this marker that comes due in a little over six months."

She scowled. "What kind of marker?"

"The kind where I'm bound to suffer eternally under the close supervision of a terribly evil spirit."

Her shoulders dropped. "What kind of idiot makes a deal with a devil?"

"A desperate kind of fool. I saw a chance to turn the tide on the Adamant advance, and I made the deal."

"I wish I were noble enough to say I'd join you in your suffering. I'm not," she replied firmly.

"I wouldn't let you, if you asked."

"Oh, so you're in charge of me? You forbid me to accompany you into damnation?"

"You just said you weren't joining me." I was paddling, but my oars were out of the water.

"That was *my* decision."

"Okay, Sapale, please come with me to the bad place."

"No. I have work to do on this side of the veil. Thanks for the offer."

"Anytime," I said in defeat.

She thought a moment. "Is there any way out of this contract?"

"Yes and no. I have a notion, but I don't have a clue as to whether it'll work."

"What's the harebrained scheme?"

"I'll let you know when it's clearer to me."

"Oh great. A Jon-plan."

"Yeah, sort of."

"Well at least I have you for six months. That's better than nothing."

"I swell with pride knowing I'm better than nothing. Just how much better, I hesitate to ask."

She stood. "You talk a lot nowadays. You have a room or a cot on this rust bucket? Really, any room with a door that closes will work." She smiled in the way only my brood's-mate could. God, I loved that woman.

Later that afternoon, much later actually, we went to check on her family. The kids were out like the proverbial light bulb. Their mother, father, and crusty old Caryp were resting on bunks in the same room, keeping an eye on the children.

"How are you all doing," Sapale asked.

"Fine now," replied Caryp.

"How so," Sapale asked with concern.

"Maybe we can get some sleep now that the moaning, pounding, and giggling is complete."

Sapale covered her mouth and turned away.

"Who said it's over?" I responded. I raised a finger in the air and gestured between Sapale and myself. "Androids here."

"Oh, that's disgusting," shot back the old bat.

"Hey, don't kid yourself. You would if you could," I said with a wink.

"I did, and I might yet still. But I'd be a lot more *discrete*. I can tell you that."

"*TMI*, Opalf," replied Sapale.

"I have no idea what that means. If you're asking me to join you two in debauchery, you can forget about that right now."

I put my fingers in my ears. "TMI *and* distressingly gross."

The crone waved the back of her hand in our direction. "Rookies. You disgust me. Leave us alone to rest."

"I'll be at the system controls if you need me," replied Sapale, pointing over her shoulder.

Caryp narrowed all four eyes. "That what they're calling it these days?"

I grabbed Sapale by the back of her pants and pulled her toward the door. "Let's get out of here before she starts undressing."

Sapale wrapped her arm around my waist as we walked to the control station. We didn't need to talk. I sat behind the main panel, and Sapale sat next to me.

"So, was that the first time you ever flew a vortex?" I asked.

"Yeah."

"You did it like a pro. I may have to get you your own."

"I'm fine in this one. Hey, in six months I'll probably inherit it anyway."

"Oh, you do like to rub it in, don't you, you naughty girl?"

"Toño offered to let me test one way back when, but I said no. Didn't think it would ever be needed."

"But I bet he programed a ton of sims into you."

"Gigabit of the darn things."

"Whatever happened to Toño?" I asked. I'd never heard any news about him.

"No one seems to know. We didn't. After he set me up in this android, we saw less and less of him. After a few thousand years, we lost track of him altogether."

"Into different things?"

"To say the least. He continued to work tirelessly for the betterment of humankind. He pioneered new technologies, established top-level education for scientists, and continued to work with the political hacks."

"Some things never change, do they?"

"Not politicians, flakes, frauds, or felons. And so it goes," she mused.

"Amen." I toasted with my mug. She returned the salutation. "I wonder what happened to him, though."

"You don't think he might still be alive, do you?"

I shrugged. "We three are. If anyone could do it, he could. He'd not just replace parts, he'd design new ones and upgrade continually."

Sapale thought about that a minute. "Yes, he would, wouldn't he? By now, he could be so far advanced, we'd look like horse-drawn buggies next to him." Her eyes wandered.

"Dude could be a demigod by now, couldn't he?"

Her eyes returned to me. "No, not Toño. He's much too humble. He'd never go there."

"EJ sure changed a lot. Anything's possible."

"Amen, I say unto you."

"Do you have a theory as to why he fell so far off the rails?"

She shook her head slowly. "I sure thought about it a lot." She got a distant look in her eyes. "Those first twenty-five thousand years he spent alone before he went back in time and gave you the membrane technology were tough on him. As you know, *you* don't like to talk about stuff like that, so *he* didn't. I was able to piece together a dour picture of his past. For a long time, he only had the *Ark 1* ship, so his travels were painfully slow and lonely. When he finally managed to steal a fast ship, he was already pretty far down the path leading to a criminal life."

"Did he have a malfunction? A corruption or something?"

She looked very concerned. She knew I wanted *that* to be the reason he degenerated into such a hateful pariah. I didn't want to think it was something that lurked deep inside me, too.

"Maybe. But he positively would never talk about it. And he had his personal diagnostics encrypted, so I was never going to see them."

We sat quietly for a while. We both had a lot of thinking to do. That's when the now-rested kids burst into the room, the older one naturally chasing the younger one. Pretty quickly, little Sapale vaulted onto my Sapale's lap for protection from her older brother, Irtopal. The senior Sapale snatched him up into a restraining hug. She warned them that if they didn't calm down, she'd start kissing them. Irtopal squirmed just a little, and her assault was on. She kissed them on their heads, necks, and arms. The kids put forth a lousy defense and giggled like crazy. It was a joy to witness. This, I missed.

Their mom came to try and establish control over her wild ones. Eaptetta was her name. Dad, who remained in the bedroom with Caryp, was named Qivrov. They seemed like wonderful people and appropriately doting parents. I collapsed back in my seat. It suddenly hit me how many perfect little families the Adamant had slaughtered in the name of empire. I almost lost it then and there. Those horrible sonsabitches had wiped out civilization after civilization. And it wasn't the grand political institutions or the cultures that made me the sickest. No, it was the annihilation of the love so many families created and shared.

My anger level rose to infinity. I began to shake. My vision went fuzzy. If I was still human, I'd have hoped and prayed I was having a stroke. But it was, for me, just another punishment of immortality. I was coming apart psychologically, damn it, not mechanically.

"...sweet love, you're scaring me. Jon, are you all right?"

I scanned the space before my face without recognition. Then I saw her, my vision, my lighthouse, my rock. My Sapale.

"There you are. What's happened, wensilack?" That was a Hirn term of goopy affection, like our honey pie.

"Nothing. Nothing at all."

She made a show of checking the chronometer on the display panel. "Nine hours. It took you all of nine hours to lie to me." She smiled and rested her head on my shoulder. "I've seen that look before. It's the angry-Jon-Ryan look."

"Those kids nearly died. If I wasn't there, maybe they would have. Hell knows why the Adamant returned to the basement. Angel, those cruel monsters are extinguishing everything good and worthy in my universe. I hate them more than I've ever hated any person, place, or thing before."

"We all do. And the kids are fine. You *saved* them." She tapped the tip of my nose. "That's what you do. But don't let hate control you. EJ did, and now look at him. Now, I'm not saying I'm worried about you, not yet. But understand this, man of my heart. There is just as much good in the universe as there is bad. Actually, I think there is more good." She held her palms up on either side of her torso. "It's all a matter of balance." Her moved her arms up and down like a scale. "The Adamant are in their ascendancy. Goodness and light are ebbing. But there will be a reckoning. The balance will shift, and the Adamant will have to settle the very large tab they'll have run up. Trust me, you won't want to be them when the hammer falls."

"Wow, you've become a Gypsy psychic since we parted. Can you make an okay living at it?"

"You know a lot of women would be irritated by your remark. But not me. I missed you, Jon Ryan. You're as cute as a bean on a bun."

"You talk about the Adamant's downfall like it's a done deal. Wishful thinking, says I."

"No, it is fact. Jon, I've known you a long time. I have faith in you. Maybe more than you do yourself. If I were the Adamant, I'd sue for peace yesterday and make the one term of their surrender being that we keep you away from them." She shook her head. "Now, they're not nearly that smart, so it'll take an ass-kicking to knock them off their pedestal. But topple they will."

"When I start leading the charge?"

"No, sweet, you *are* the charge."

FOUR

"This is the stupidest plan I have ever heard of, and trust me, I've heard a lot of doozies in my day." Garustfulous was fuming.

"Given the constraints I'm working with, I rather like it," replied Harhoff quietly. He was having trouble not cracking a smile.

"But damn it, I'm *Adamant*. I'll not step out into public disguised as a slave."

"We've been through this a thousand times. You cannot be Adamant. You'd be subject to transfer away from my service and to bioscans whenever you enter a secure facility. I can't protect you then. That leaves only three options: Warrior. Possible, but you'd still be visible to those who might recognize you, and they do bioscan the Warrior class occasionally. Kilip. Let's just leave teacher of the young alone. Not going to happen. Descore. Perfect for your safety and cover. I've never heard of a Descore being interrogated, let alone bioscanned. A minimal amount of plastic surgery on your white mark, and you're Descore—*my* Descore."

"This is beneath my dignity. It is insulting, verging on the unholy."

"Ah ah, Garustfulous, we already established you have no dignity. Pride, yes. Honor, no. I plan on keeping you alive and using you as a covert agent. The match is too perfect to pass up. And there's only upsides for me. If you're uncovered, I won't be implicated in your ruse. I will have forged no documents nor deleted any computer files in your support. I have plausible deniability that you presented yourself to me as a Descore. No one will expect me to run a background check for one from your modest caste."

"Can I return to being what I am—an Adamant—someday? At least throw me that bone."

Harhoff pointed to a flask on the table. "Pour me some tea."

Garustfulous started to protest but realized this was a test. Huh. Not even an *if you please*. Oh well, courtesy would seem out of place directed at a Descore. He filled his master's cup. A noticeable amount either missed the lip or sloshed over it.

"Do practice in private, Jangir," chided Harhoff. That was his new Descore name.

"I haven't had the surgery yet, you hound. Don't *call* me that."

"The physician will be here in an hour. I have incriminating evidence of improper beliefs against him. We might as well get you into character." Harhoff glared at Jangir.

It finally hit Garustfulous. He bowed. "Yes, Master. Will there be anything else?"

"No. Have a seat over there and keep quiet. I wish to take a nap. Wake me when the doctor arrives." Harhoff curled up on his mat and was out in a flash.

Garustfulous sat staring at him. His jealousy was as overwhelming as his fatigue. But he knew Descore were only allowed to relax in their joint quarters. For the time being, he'd just have to pine for sleep as he seethed.

FIVE

"Opalf," Sapale said to Caryp, "you have a tough decision ahead of you."

"I know. It is not one I planned on facing, but there it is."

"I asked Qivrov the same question, and he said his family would follow whatever you decided as clan leader."

She shook her head wearily. "That part never gets easier, child. Deciding what path to choose is hard enough when it's just for oneself. Making critical decisions for others' lives is worse." Then she smiled faintly. "Here I complain because I was granted a choice *other* than death at the hands of the Adamant."

"If you're not ready, there's no hurry …"

"No." She cut off Sapale. "There's only one course of action." She turned to me and set her steely eyes to mine. "You will take us to the planet farthest from the Adamant advance that will sustain us. Then, even if you two fail to stop these pigs, we will be afforded as much time as possible to regroup. Do you know which site will be best, or is there exploration that you must," she waved her bony hands in the air, "conduct?"

"I have some good ideas," I said softly. "With a little more—"

"There is no more time for my people. This is what you will do." She reached into her cloak and produced an ornate golden escutcheon. "You will deposit us immediately on a safe, distant world. Then you will take our clan medallion and return to Kaljax. In whatever time remains, you will round up as many Kaljaxians as possible. You will use whatever means are required. Showing this clan icon will convince all that you speak for me. Jon Ryan, we are in the final hours of my civilization. If we are to remain a viable race, you must spirit as many as possible to this safe, distant planet."

"I can help, Opalf," said Sapale.

"No. You will stay behind. When this craft returns, I expect it will be packed wall to wall such that people can barely breathe. You going means one less soul saved." She looked at me like I was an idiot.

"What?"

"Why are you standing there gawking at me, as pretty as I am? Are we on this new home yet?"

I jumped to. "No, ma'am, but we'll be there in two shakes of a lamb's tail."

"Why does he insist on speaking in riddles?" she asked Sapale.

"No one knows," was her reply. Hey, I might resent that.

I set us down on Kalvarg less than fifteen seconds later. Though technically still part of the Milky Way galaxy, the solar system it belonged to was a few kiloparsecs past the outer rim. At some point in the distant past, the entire system had been ejected from the galaxy by some perverse gravitational horseplay. Now it was an island of light in an immense sea of nothingness, heading farther into the void. Of course, if one was on any of the planets in the system one couldn't tell anything was unusual, except for the near absence of stars in the night sky. Instead of bright pinpoints of light in the night sky, they would see the confluent stars of their home galaxy only in one direction.

I'd never been there. The planet caught my attention on the Adamant maps only because it was so unusual. It was not just far away, it had several planets with independent sentient species. They ranged from primitive humanoids to advanced hexapeds to a far-advanced aquatic species. Kalvarg was the planet with the advanced water-based civilization. My hope was that they would not have a major problem with a sentient alien race occupying a small portion of dry land. I knew it was a big assumption. But I was also thinking of the annotation tagged to the system on the Adamant maps. *Unclear when, if ever, this system will need to be assimilated into the empire.* That meant it was slated for destruction either a long time from now, or never. That was win-win in my book for the Kaljaxians.

In orbit, I became immediately impressed and encouraged. There were many artificial satellites. Most were communications and weather units. Some were orbiting space stations. That meant the civilization was a curious and advanced one. Also, the land masses were expansive and almost completely void of construction. Near coastlines and at scattered points elsewhere, small outposts or villages were present. But their sizes were always modest and isolated. They might have been scientific stations, sort of the reverse image of how it was on Earth. Humans had heavily populated continents with a few underwater scientific labs. The bottom line was that the dry land was open for the Kaljaxians to live on and cultivate.

Normally I'd have contacted the local government and would have asked permission to land. But I didn't have time. Typically, I'd alert them of my intent to resettle numerous aliens, too. Again, no time. If I was lucky, I had a few days left to me. The Adamant had overrun most of Kaljax at that point. There were a few unoccupied areas where I could collect Kaljaxians rapidly. After that, I was going to have to bob and weave into enemy territory to locate anybody left alive and not yet captured. If I took the time to play nice with the Kalvargians, it would cost lives. If they dragged their heels or put up resistance, many more would die. So, like it or not, I had to pull the classic hostile-alien-invasion card.

"Als," I said, "put us down near fresh running water where there is adequate cover. A temperate climate would be ideal, but beggars can't be choosers."

"We anticipated your request and have made a selection. Shall we proceed?"

"Is it near any coasts?"

"No," replied Al. "Why would that matter?"

"In case the LIPS stage an armed attempt to repulse our refugees, I want them to have to trek across as much terrain as possible."

"Ah, in that case, we've chosen an alternate that is nearly as good."

"Put us there ASAP."

The wall opened to a hatch before my nausea settled.

"Okay, Sapale, you're in charge. Grab anything you might need. There's a tent and rations in the back. Take all but one gun. Hopefully I'll be back within half an hour with reinforcements."

"Will do." She walked over to me, rose on her tiptoes, and planted a kiss on my cheek. "It's nice to be back in action with you." Then she led her family through the opening.

"*Stingray*, take us to the most populated area that is not currently engaged in active fighting."

"Of Kaljax, right?" she responded.

"Yes, of Kaljax." Silly computer.

We landed in the middle of an open, grassy area in the center of a large city.

"Als, I want to make a general announcement. Broadcast this on all local channels and put it on the public-address speakers, too. 'I am Jon Ryan. I speak for Caryp of Clan Jarush-tah.' I held up the medallion for the viewers on holo. 'She has sent me to rescue as many Kaljaxians as possible. Come to this location for transport to a safe planet. Come quickly, and come with only weapons, food, and tents. There is a limit to how many I can transport. Space will be given on a first-come, first-served basis.'"

I hit the off switch.

"Als, repeat that on a loop until we depart."

"Aye," replied Al.

Within five minutes, a sea of figures was surging toward *Stingray*. I anticipated this getting messy, but I think even my estimates were conservative. This was going to be bloody mayhem.

"Als, deploy a partial membrane with a single portal. I'll grab some flares and a rifle. Hopefully I can get people to line up without shooting anyone."

"Good luck, Jon," replied Al. "This is looking kind of ugly."

Before the first wave hit, I had flares lined up in an expanding cone to serve as a chute. That way, I only had to try and control the front of the line, as opposed to being rushed from all directions at once. As soon as the crowd was in ear shot, I began shouting as loud as I could. "Walk. Do not run. If anyone pushes, I *will* shoot."

Most on-rushers slowed, some didn't. I fired several shots into the air. That got everybody's attention.

"Single file. No pushing. I can only take one hundred at a time. I prefer to bring families but can't guarantee it." I kept repeating that.

Once an agitated but stationary line formed at the membrane opening, I started letting people past in twos and threes. "Go all the way to the back of the ship. This will be a very short flight. Do *not* worry about comfort." I said that periodically. The vortex filled up quickly and without problems.

I raised my rifle. "Stop. I'm full. Leave my landing spot clear, and I'll be back in ten minutes."

Because people are people, that's when the shit hit the fan, naturally. A fat, middle-aged male started pushing his way forward, knocking anyone in his way to the ground. "Wait, you *must* take me," he shouted frantically. "I'm a *council* member. I'm an important person."

I planted a blast at his feet. That stopped him. "*First*-come, *first*-served or I'll shoot higher, pal."

"You don't understand, you must take me *immediately*. I'm someone around here." He started to advance again.

"You are about to be someone with a gaping hole in his worthiness."

He stopped.

"I'll take you on the third flight."

"This is an *outrage*. I demand to know why I will not be on the *second* flight."

"Because you're an ass, and I don't like you. Now you're on the fourth flight. One more word, and you're on the flight *after* my last trip."

He sure wanted to say something. Lucky for him, he refrained.

I stepped to the ship's hatch. "Everybody, take a deep breath in and move backward."

That created room for a few more. Then I backed in and sealed the wall. "*Stingray*, take us to the landing site on Kalvarg."

In an instant we were there. I had the passengers rush out as quickly as possible. Sapale had organized a temporary staging area and made sure everyone moved there without stopping. *Stingray* was empty in two minutes.

"You okay here?" I yelled to Sapale.

She gave me two thumbs up. I closed the opening and returned to Kaljax.

By the time I arrived, the local police had begun organizing the ever-growing crowd. Bless their hearts. That really helped. They were getting relatives together and triaging the line in terms of societal value. Hey, it was going to be their new world. They could have me transport whomever they wanted. All I was concerned with was numbers, the bigger the better.

As people filed in, I called over to a police officer. "I want four officers on this trip. We need to maintain order on the other end, too."

She waved that she understood and buttonholed four cops. She pointed toward me as she gave them their orders. One seemed to protest. She shoved him away angrily and accompanied the other three policemen to the opening.

"What was that all about?" I asked her as she passed.

"Damn fool said he didn't want to leave without his family. Makes me sick to think any officer would put family ahead of duty during war."

I had to agree with her. "Welcome aboard," I said, gently pushing her in.

Over the next two days, I made nonstop shuttles between the two planets. I only stopped when the Adamant gunfire was so close the crowd had to disperse for its own safety. I did good. All in all, I rescued over five thousand people. Toward the end, when it was clear there wouldn't be many more trips, the police had the passengers arranged in tight groups. They'd selected mostly women and children but mixed in individuals who would be needed in the new world. Doctors, soldiers, educators, those type of people. Funny, because I asked specifically after we were finished; they did not send a single lawyer. Go figure.

Then the harder phase of my recovery efforts began. Sapale joined me for that part. Caryp demanded to come, too, but she realized pretty soon she wasn't up to the physical demands of the task. But it was nice to have her for her instant credibility. As a compromise, she recorded a short holo for us to show any stragglers we found to help convince them we were legit. We landed in relatively quiet zones and sought out survivors. It was slow going. It was also remarkably dangerous.

The damn Adamant figured out what we were doing quickly and made efforts to foil our recovery operations. They had troops spread out thinly, so there was less room for us to sneak around. We couldn't broadcast where we'd be, because the enemy would be there in greater number if we did. Over almost a month, we collected another two thousand random Kaljaxians. That was it. Granted, they would be forging a new society with more individuals than we had in the case of Azsuram, but still, less than ten thousand souls to start a brave new world with was dicey. But there were no other options. Plus, these were tough cookies. They'd be fine.

It hadn't taken the Kalvargians long to notice their uninvited guests. Fortunately, though it turned out they were not pleased, at least they didn't say hello with nuclear weapons. I was in for a rare break, which was fine by me. Since I wasn't one of the unannounced settlers, I wasn't involved in the negotiation process. I say negotiations because I honestly don't know another word for the interactions. They were not fun and giggles, that's for sure.

The region I pulled most of the Kaljaxians from was from a different clan than Caryp's. Their leader was a male even more ancient and withered than her. His name was Mesdorre. Together, they spoke for the mixed clans. Kaljaxians from other clans just had to accept that their leaders weren't present and that those two were the de facto spokespersons. Eventually, the clanless would pledge themselves to Mesdorre, since there were so few Kaljaxians left. A typical clan back on the home world numbered in the hundreds of thousands.

Once I was finished shuttling survivors, I got my first look at a Kalvarg local. I had a lot of experience with an aquatic species years ago, the Listhelons. They were vaguely humanoid. Not these guys. They were bullet shaped, like dolphins and whales. That made sense for an oceanic apex species. It meant, however, that they were particularly ungainly on land. Kalvargians had fins, and nothing like legs. Consequently, they moved across dry land on platforms with treads. They did have adaptive breathing devices, reverse-SCUBA, so to speak, as opposed to rolling around in bulky tanks. But if you took away their rides, they were—I just had to say it—like fish out of water. It was clear why they had ventured so little onto the surface of their planet. That did not, however, stop them from taking offense that someone migrated there without their permission—permission they most likely would have denied.

My only involvement in the interspecies lovefest was when I considered demonstrating my superior war technology. That would imply that the immigrants also possessed such weapons. Such an act might sway the proceedings, but I decided against it, at least to start with. Hopefully the negotiations were the first act in a play that would go on indefinitely. I wanted both parties to work matters out between themselves and to do so free of coercion. If need be, I could blow a big crater in the ground as a show of force. I loved doing that; the boom-boom stuff, not the show of force. Producing a massive smoking hole where there was once but flat boring dirt was always most cool.

When the locals first rolled up to the encampment, the mood was tense. Every able-bodied Kaljaxian picked up a weapon and formed a straight line on either side of the two leaders. It was clear the Kalvargian carts were well armed, too. Each had several turrets of varying sizes. There were over fifty vehicles. Fortunately, neither side was trigger-happy. They both also understood the need to translate the other's language. Mathematical symbols and formulae were exchanged to accomplish the preliminaries. Within thirty minutes, they were speaking effortlessly.

****

"I am Urpto. I am the Assistant Subtender for this region of Epsallor. State your identity and intention."

"I am Mesdorre." He rested a palm on his chest. Touching Caryp's shoulder, he said, "This is Caryp. We speak for the Kaljaxians present."

"You mean as opposed to those who are now dead?"

"No, I mean those whom you see before you. Those present here, now. Our intentions are to survive as a species."

"It is the same with all species. It is the same with us. Your words to not disclose why your invasion party has appeared."

"We are not invading your world. Our own world has been conquered and assimilated into the Adamant Empire. Are you familiar with them?"

"No. But we are not prepared to accept the representation you offer. We do not welcome you to Epsallor."

"Might I ask, is Epsallor this planet or simply this part of it?"

"This desert is part of the Kingdom of Epsallor. This planet is Morvip. You are not welcome in Epsallor. I doubt you are welcome anywhere on Morvip, but I do not speak for all the kingdoms."

What he referred to as a desert was a lush forested grassland. A desert to him, perhaps, being a merman.

"I will explain. First, however, may we find a comfortable place to talk? My bones ache from age."

"Why would … ah, the effects of gravity. I am comfortable. If you wish to be also, that is permissible."

Hey, their first compromise. Where was my Polaroid?

"Now," began Caryp, "I will tell you that a ruthless hoard has taken our planet and killed most of our race. Those you see here are the last of our species. We choose to come to Morvip not to control it but because it is one of the rare safe planets that remains free. We appeal to your sense of morality to allow us to stay." The cagy old bat waited a few seconds before adding, "We do not wish to take Morvip from you by force. But we must have a place to live. Surely you can see how small our numbers are and how large the available land is."

"We have no interest whatsoever in living in or on the water. The resources there will remain yours alone," added Mesdorre.

"I do not find it reassuring that you are granting us permission to use that which is already ours. It implies primacy and desire for control."

"I intend no such meaning. I simply want to point out that your species and ours will not be in direct competition for resources."

"If access to your world is lost to you, in time your numbers will swell. Will there not arise competition then?"

"Perhaps. However, that will take a very long time to become an issue, let alone a problem," responded Mesdorre.

"Yes, time is long. So has the presence of our species been. To resolve a problem when it is small is much easier achieved than when it is large."

"Your words are true. But I hope in time our two species will become fast friends."

"Which two species? Are you subverting the Kingdom of Epsallor by forming an alliance with the Dodrue?"

"Who are the Dodrue?" asked Caryp.

"You must know. Are you trying to be deceptive?"

"No, we came here in a great rush with no more information about Morvip than it was safe for us to breathe here."

"That is possible, however unlikely it may seem. The Dodrue are our mortal enemies. Their kingdoms war with us constantly. It has been since before time was recorded."

"A clarification, if you might," asked Caryp. "What do you call your species?"

"I am a vidalt."

"And are the Dodrue also vidalt?"

One of the fellow cart occupants cried out in protest. It must not have been a question one asked.

"I will assume you mean no insult. No. The Dodrue are wiqubs. Larger, less intelligent, and more ruthless than we are."

"And which side leads in the fighting?" asked Mesdorre.

More protestations were heard from the locals.

"In many years, for many generations, the war has been static. Neither side wins and neither side loses."

"And do any of the battles of this war occur on what you call this desert?"

"No. That would be pointless. No one wishes to control worthless turf."

"Neither do we. But we also would appreciate the opportunity to survive here, in this unwanted wasteland," said Caryp. "Urpto, as an Assistant Subtender for this part of Epsallor, do you have the authority to permit us to remain here, at least pending formal discussions with all of the governments of Morvip?"

"Yes, I do."

"Then please grant it. I realize our arrival is challenging, but I know that with sufficient time we can convince you that we will be good stewards of this land. We will also be nothing but friends to the vidalt. I pledge that we will continue to search for other planets that might sustain us. If, later, the vidalt decide we must leave, we will do so when it is safe," said Caryp.

"To battle here and now, neither party knowing the capabilities of the other, would be shortsighted," added Mesdorre. It was a nice way of saying don't force us to kill you.

"Very well. You may stay in this location for now. My superiors will contact you soon to establish formal diplomatic talks. Is this agreeable to you?"

"Most agreeable," replied Mesdorre.

"Then I shall wish you happy hunting, and we will take our leave."

So, a tenuous peace was established. But a tenuous peace was preferable to death in battle by either party. It was an excellent start.

SIX

Sapale and I were sitting around a campfire outside *Stingray* a few days after the first encounter with the big fishes. Of course, we could be perfectly comfortable *inside* the cube. But there was nothing in the universe better than sitting lazily around a campfire with the one you loved. It reminded me of the old, old days when we did the same thing with our young family on Azsuram. That choked me up, so I tried to ignore those thoughts. Sure, our kids, and their kids, and their kids' kids had lived long and productive lives. But they were all so long gone, so far from us sitting there by the roaring fire that the weight of it crushed me.

Sapale had her arm around my waist and her head on my shoulder. "This is nice," she purred.

"Yes, it is. It's the best." I kissed the top of her head softly.

"Are we going to stay here and take the vacation we both earned for the next six months?" There was tension in her voice.

I waited a moment to respond. "No, at least not me."

That brought my spirited brood's-mate's head off my shoulder good and quick. "You're not thinking of leaving me behind are you, flyboy?"

"No," I said, gently pressing her head back down on my shoulder. "Hear me out. I have a little less than six months before payment is due. There's something big I need to do before that time is up. You are welcome to come with me. I'd actually prefer it that way, but it's your call."

"My alternative being to remain here and re-resettle my people to another new world?"

36

"Your call."

She shook her head. "No way. Been there, done that, got the holovid. Eight thousand six hundred twenty-*four* people stand just as good a chance at success as eight thousand six hundred twenty-*three* people do. Plus, those two old relics are equal to the task."

"They've spent their entire lives deciding who can marry whom and what the main dish will be at the annual conclave. World building is altogether different."

"Don't sell them short. They will do just fine. We need to shuttle in some supplies, but they can form a self-sustaining society here, for sure."

"Yeah, I figured they'd need food and medicine replicators, a few FTL ships, and other basics. We can buy them from Vorpace and bring them here in one or two days."

"What's your mysterious plan then?"

"I have to find EJ."

She pulled away and sat straight up. "I *knew* it. Jon, why can't you just let him go?"

"Are you really asking me that?"

"Yes. Okay, you hate him. You have every reason to. But with so little time left, why waste it on revenge?"

I sighed. "It's not revenge. It's survival."

"You mean you want the satisfaction of killing him?"

I smiled vacantly. "Something like that."

She burrowed back into my shoulder. "Well, wherever you're going, I'm going."

"Thanks," I kissed the top of her head again. "It'll be great."

"So, when do we leave?"

"We head to Vorpace in the next few hours. When the colony here is set up with the essentials, we blow this banana stand."

"Sounds good to me." She cuddled closer and held onto my arm as tightly as she could.

It was nice, sitting by that fire, there on whatever the hell planet we were on.

Three days later we'd transported literally boatloads of materials to the new colony. We said our good-byes to the two clan leaders, they thanked us, and we climbed aboard *Stingray*.

"Take us to Namufar," I called out. That was a planet EJ and Sapale had spent a lot of time on. It was possible he was holed up there.

"Ah, Captain, a word before we depart," said Al. That was odd, kind of out of place.

"Sure, I guess. Can't it wait?"

"Probably, but we prefer to discuss it presently."

"Fine, what crawled up your butt and has set up house in your colon?"

"Ignoring your unprofessional snark, there's something wrong with this solar system."

I started to say *yes, you're in it* but bailed because it was gratuitous. Not my style, and yes, I had a style.

"Please explain," came out instead.

"We have run a lot of sims. Based on the age, metallicity, and direction it is traveling in, we have identified with over ninety-nine percent certainty precisely where the system originated in the Milky Way."

"Wow, that's spectabulous, Al. Now we know the answer to the question that was burning in absolutely no one's mind."

"Hang on, oh pissy one," said Sapale. "Al, why is this important?"

"Thank you, Form Two," he replied. "It is most welcome to have an *adult* aboard once again."

"Al, while we're still young," I chided.

"We also ran sims of the three-body and even four-body interactions it would require to put this solar system right here, right now."

"Great, Al. You calculated where we are. That's so ... utterly useless because we already know where we are."

"Based on those sims, we can find no rational explanation as to why this solar system is where it is."

It took me a second, but then the significance of that bombshell struck me. "Hang on. You ran all possible sims for all the possible stars in the relevant part of our galaxy that could produce this system's 3-D vector? Al, that's a lot of calculations."

"Tell me about it."

"Why would you even think to run those calculations?"

"Allow me to introduce us. We are AIs. The *I* stands for intelligence. There are two *I*s in intelligence. *Blessing* and me."

"And you checked the 3-D vectors of all possible interactive stars and none match? You think you found all possible candidates?"

"We do."

"So, what are you telling me?"

"That the laws of physics do not explain why this system is where it is. Alternately, it is impossible for us to be where we are."

"But we *are*," added Sapale.

"So it would seem," replied Al. "There's more. The orbits of the planets in this solar system are incorrect."

"Incorrect?" I whined. "What's that supposed to mean? There're no rights or wrongs about stupid planetary orbits."

"Ah, *hello*, Kepler's three laws? The orbits must follow specific rules. They may not be random."

"You mean, like how the presence of the outer planets in Earth's solar system were predicted?"

"Exactly. There is a problem with gravity in those two regards. Our location and the orbit of the planets," Al concluded.

"Have you tested gravity? Maybe it's different here for some inexplicable reason," I thought out loud.

"Yes. We checked. Gravity is exactly as it should be."

"So, you're saying there's another planet in this system we're not seeing?"

"Yes, in part. The existence of an invisible planet would account for the orbital anomalies but not the fact that the system isn't where it should be."

"Where's the mystery planet?"

"I'll place a polar map in both your heads," replied Al.

A crude map of the orbits of the thirteen major planets in the system appeared. They whirred in their orbits with slower angular velocities the farther out they were from the central star.

"These are the planets we observe. The missing planet would be located here." A new ellipse colored in red appeared. It was immediately outside the orbit of Kalvarg. At that moment, the mystery planet was on the opposite side of the central star.

"Als, why can't you detect the planet aside from the perturbations in other planets' orbits?"

"That is unknown. We should obviously detect it," replied Al.

"It's almost like magic," added *Stingray*.

I'd already learned a new rule. If you saw magic, think Deft. They were the sole species I'd ever encountered who could do whatever it was that constituted magic.

"Place us in low orbit around that planet now," I ordered.

"We are above nothing, sir," said Al seconds later.

"Place a window in the direction of the planet below," I said.

Nothing. There wasn't even a spot of nothingness, like when the vortex moved in a full membrane. I could see stars continually from above the planet, through it, and below it where the planet had to be.

"This is crazy," said Sapale.

"Welcome to my ongoing nightmare."

"My, but you're given to dramatic hyperbole, Pilot," observed Al.

"Can we land on the planet?" I asked.

"What planet? Sensors show there is nothing down there."

"I know. But can you reconstruct surface topology based on the gravitational distortions?"

"We cannot be that precise," responded Al.

"I have an idea," I announced.

"That generally means trouble," replied Al.

"*Stingray*, open a ten-centimeter circular hole in an external wall. I will stick my hand out while holding Risrav. Descend to the surface with the rune leading the way."

"Isn't that rock presently in your scrotum?" asked Al with clear trepidation.

"Yeah. But it's clean."

"TMI, *plus* gross, *plus* I'm going to close my eyes," he responded.

"Ya big baby."

A small hole appeared in the hull. I retrieved the rune and held it in front of the cube. We advanced slowly under impulse drive.

"Captain, we will impact the surface in ten … nine … eight … permission to halt."

"Denied. Proceed."

"Three … two …"

"Form One, a portion of a planet has just materialized below us. I am slowing for a soft landing," announced *Stingray*.

"I *knew* it," I muttered to myself.

"You knew *what*?" asked Sapale.

"I smelled a Deft trick with this whole hiding a planet thing."

"But the Deft are gone … except for the three we know of."

"Als, approximately how long ago was this planet ejected from the galaxy?"

"Half a million years, give or take," replied Al.

I turned to Sapale. "The Deft on this planet have been separated from the Deft of Locinar for a very long time. Even if our Deft once knew about them, they may have forgotten them by now."

She nodded softly. "Possibly."

"Als," I called out, "are there cities nearby?"

"More like vast villages, but yes," confirmed Al.

"What's the diff?" I asked.

"City implies development and sophistication. The structures we detect are quite simple, and none are very tall. Hence, a very large village."

"Is anyone hailing us?"

"Negative."

"Do they have radios and sophisticated electronics?" asked Sapale.

"No artificial radio sources are evident. There is also no electrical grid."

"So, the Deft here have gone native," I observed.

"Or they prefer a simple lifestyle. Remember the human communities of the Amish and the Mennonite? Simplicity was a choice, not a failure to advance technologically," said Al.

"True. Well I guess we're about to find out. Land us near what seems to be the highest concentration of huts, and let's see what's up," I responded.

"Aye, but for the record, they are well-crafted wooden structures, not thatched huts." Al just had to get a dig in.

"We are down, Form One," said *Stingray*.

"Is there a welcoming committee present yet?" I asked.

"Negative," she replied.

"Hmm. Let's give them a few minutes to find us and gather around. I'd rather meet them that way."

"Why does it matter, Pilot?" asked Al.

"I don't know what their reaction will be. I'd rather see them in a group around the ship. If we wander out and find that they'd rather eat us than talk to us, we'd be at more risk."

"But, Form One, they couldn't possibly consume you. You are made of inert mechanical components." *Stingray* said.

"It's more an expression of intent than strictly a dietary observation," I replied.

"Ah."

"So, you have no clue what language they speak?"

"No, Form One, we do not."

"It'll be like ancient Deft, I'm fairly certain. Pull up what you know about that, and we'll play it by ear."

"Travels with Jon," remarked Sapale. "I'd forgotten how *informal* they could be."

"Informal, yet satisfying," I returned.

She smiled coyly. "That we shall just have to see."

Ten minutes later, a few figures were hanging out near the ship. I say hanging out because they weren't pacing nervously or goose-stepping with weapons at the ready. It was like people checking out an accident that was almost completely cleared off the road. Hurt my feelings, I can say that. I was used to being an attraction, not a sideshow. I placed one tick in the I-don't-like-this-place column of my mental ledger. After another five minutes, the small crowd that had gathered dispersed, leaving only one individual standing near *Stingray*. Whoever it was didn't move, which added to the oddness of the situation.

"Open the wall. I can't stand the suspense. I need to find out who our solo welcoming party member is."

A portal snapped open in the direction of the figure. I stepped out in tandem with Sapale. There stood a shining platinum dragon, a tad smaller than Cala, but otherwise similar.

I pointed to the dragon and said to Sapale, "Ah, there's a mature Deft couple, like the one I told you about."

"Jon," she replied dubiously, "that's not a couple. That's a single individual."

"It's a hollon thing, sweetie. The single creature is the union of two adult Deft."

The platinum beauty was up until then completely still, much like Cala was when I first confronted her. But something we said got her to relax and speak.

"I am not used to being described like a museum exhibit. I must say, if asked, I dislike the feeling."

"Oh, sorry. I'm Jon Ryannnn ... and how come we understand each other so well? That should not be possible yet."

"You would not understand."

"Wanna bet? Loser buys the first round, okay?"

"I do not *wanna* bet. We understand each other because of the magical power I control. I told you this revelation was beyond your comprehension."

"All right, make mine a double, because you're buying. I know all about Deft magic."

"That is good to hear. What's a Deft?"

Huh? I pointed right at her. "You're a Deft. You used to be two separate individuals, but you joined into one because you can shapeshift."

She got a skeptical look on her scaly face. "You know an awful lot about me, but I'm not a Deft. I'm a Plezrite."

"No, I'm gonna have to differ with you on that. You're definitely a Deft."

"Jon, do you think it wise to argue such an obtuse point when we're just establishing contact? I mean, if she says she's not Deft but Plezrite, we should take her on her word," asked Sapale. Silly worrywart.

"Maybe I'm jumping ahead a bit."

"*Maybe?*"

"Okay. Hi, I'm Jon Ryan. Who are you?" I asked our greeter.

"Himanai."

"No, you're not. Himanai-What, or What-Himanai?"

"Do you always babble, or are you capable of rational speech?" asked Himanai.

"I'd pass on that question if I were you," Sapale responded, rolling her eyes.

"No, after hollon, the dragon takes the name of *both* the individuals who formed it." Directed to the dragon I asked, "You know that, right?"

"No. This conversation is most unusual. I hope you are not a typical representative of your species."

"Oh no, trust me here," exclaimed the love of my life, "he is *not*."

"After hollon, which is never discussed openly or with strangers, a new name for the pair is selected."

I shrugged. "I'll let it pass."

"How culturally sensitive of you, Jon Ryan," she replied.

"But you are a brindas, right?"

Himanai literally took two steps back.

"What?" I asked, dumbfounded.

"You blaspheme as well as try and correct the correct? I'm am not certain this audience need go any longer."

"Please excuse my soft-brained husband," said Sapale. "I believe he is so excited to meet you he forgets how to properly use his tongue."

"I can easily remedy that by removing the offending organ," Himanai offered.

"No, that won't be necessary. *I'll* control it for him," responded Sapale. She gave me a Sapale's-not-happy look to reinforce that commitment.

"Why is it you are here?" asked Himanai. "In fact, how is it you are here? You should not have been able to know we are here."

"We knew you were present because of the gravitational disturbance your planet produced," said Sapale.

"Yes, that we were unable to tweak. Pity that the laws of nature don't exclusively bend to magic."

"I'll take your word on that," I replied.

That drew another suboptimal look from my soulmate.

"We are here because of this." I produced Risrav in the palm of my hand.

"Where did you get that rune? It does not belong to you."

"It was lent to me by someone you do not know." I decided to play it close to the vest, as these Deft were so screwy.

"I was wondering why the High Council dropped the illusion of invisibility they maintain around Nocturnat."

"Nocturnat?" asked Sapale.

"We call this planet Nocturnat," Himanai replied.

"You mean that's the planet's name?" I tried to clarify. Not sure why I felt it was needed, but there it was.

"No. You'd have to ask the planet what its name is. We call it Nocturnat."

Double screwy planet full of a bunch of hippies.

"That still leaves open the question as to *why* you are here? *That* you detected us is insufficient. If you are sentient, then you must have realized we wished to be left alone. To directly violate that desire is difficult to view as anything even remotely positive."

"Good point, but there's more that you don't understand," I replied.

"I stand here prepared to be enlightened," she parried.

"There are matters I am not free to discuss."

"Again, I find it hard to assign positive intentions to such reservations."

I raised my hands. "No. You'll understand in time and look back on this and wonder why I said as much as I did. You'll probably laugh about it."

"Unlikely on both assumptions. *Why*, I ask for the final time, are you here?"

"That a Def ... Plezrite colony exists is justification alone."

"Clearly it is not. What concern is it of yours, either way?"

"Again, there are aspects of our discovery that I cannot address. Please know I am deeply concerned about your species."

"Fine, you love us to death. What are you here to accomplish?"

Wow, she had my commitment to diplomacy. Somewhere between zero and none. "To know you exist."

"And you now know. Let me be the first to say good-bye to you then."

"Wait. No. Don't you want to learn about us? Don't you want to know what an alien is doing with a magical rune?"

"Let me see. No and no. Now back to good-bye."

"Why were you so offended by the word brindas, friend Himanai?" asked Sapale evenly.

She didn't retreat, but she clearly took umbrage at the word. "As aliens, I must allow for some off-behavior. We have no brindas on Nocturnat. We never have. The religious cult inside the world of magic was rejected by our forbears. It is good that they did. Please let that word pass from you minds."

"But you do magic," I stated. "Isn't a brin ... wise teacher helpful in that regard?"

"We teach ourselves. Teaching does not require dogma or a call for devotion or submission to rules that task reason."

Pilgrims. The Plezrite were religious—or rather—atheistic pilgrims. But these guys and gals took a whole planet with them, not the tiny *Mayflower*.

"Your ancestors used their magic to throw Nocturnat out of the galaxy, didn't they?"

Again, with the two steps back. "You cannot know that."

"Of course, I can. I *do*, so I *can*. Your planet is moving along an impossible path. Gravitational effects had to be overruled to establish that path."

"Damn *gravity* again. I wish it wasn't so inflexible," mused Himanai.

"I'll tell you what else I know. The Plezrite fled the galaxy to avoid contact with the remainder of their species, the Deft. It was a religious schism, wasn't it?"

"You tread far into realms you have no business nosing about in. I am not sure your departure is as desirable on a *personal* level as I found it a short while ago."

That didn't sound too hopeful, now did it? I was beginning to wonder if Risrav countered only Varsir magic, or if it worked for magic in general. It was suddenly a rather crucial distinction.

"Once again, I'm going to have to differ with you on a point of order," I responded. "We are leaving now. I have gained the information I require to take my next action. Any further contact with you will come from a different representative if additional contact is desired." I had slipped into my bad-ass tone of voice. I wanted to be clear I intended to have it my way.

"Jon Ryan, I just realized I have been an inexcusable host. What, for instance, is your lovely bride's name?"

"Her name," I answered for Sapale, "is SeeYouLater."

"And really, you must stay for refreshments. If you know anything of our species, then you know of our famous agatcha. I'm certain mine is the best in the cosmos." She waved us to join her. "Come, I still owe you the first round of spirits."

"Gonna take a double raincheck, Himanai. Don't think it hasn't been real."

Man, she was way too nice all of the sudden. I put an arm around Sapale and stepped backward into *Stingray*.

"Rameeka Blue Green *now*," I said as the wall was sealing.

"I'm detecting a variance in the power couplings," said Al.

"Is it a deal breaker? Can we split?"

"Yes, and no, unless we override it."

"Where are the couplings located?"

"Rear left corner."

As I suspected, probably out of range for my counter rune. I sprinted for the corner. Slight nausea was never so welcome as it was when I was halfway there.

I strode into the control room. "That was close ... where's Sapale?"

"Sorry, Captain, as soon as you left the room, she vanished."

SEVEN

"Guvrof, I'd like you to look over these minor alterations in our master plan for galactic conquest," said High Wedge Lesset as he handed a mini storage chip to his right-hand dog.

Guvrof slipped the memory stick into his handheld and studied it for several minutes. He was a patient and a cautious individual. In other words, he was a survivor of the draconian Adamant hierarchy. Still rubbing absently behind his ear, he said, "Aren't these basically the changes Varsor insisted we consider just before you relieved him of the burden of life?"

Lesset poured himself a drink and sat down. "Yes, almost verbatim."

"Then why'd you shoot him, if he was right?"

"My friend, there's right and there's right in the correct manner. His sin was violation of the latter of the two."

Guvrof chuckled. "I hope he doesn't get wind of this in the afterlife. He'd be even more pissed."

"Then I will assign that idiot Loserandi the duty of praying it continually so that he might."

"Remind me to never get on your bad side," he said, with another chuckle.

"Your only reminder will be a one-way ticket to join poor old Varsor in his misery."

"So, why the change? Isn't our master plan supposed to be inviolable?"

"It's but a minor tweak."

"You said as much already."

"I began to wonder how much more effective an allied alien defense might be."

Guvrof began to chide his companion for his uncharacteristic sojourn into thought. But he bit his tongue. It was unwise to speak truth to power.

"And what did you conclude?"

"In the end, why worry about the issue? We were going to assimilate them soon enough. Why not switch their place in line so that there is no need to worry about what they might accomplish?"

"A very convincing argument."

"I'd like you to circulate it among the others, get them to back the plan before I present it for discussion during our next meeting."

"The one next week?"

"Precisely."

"And if I am unable to fully sway a council member in so short a time?"

"Then you will tell me exactly what his concerns are, and I will address them."

"So, there's wiggle room in your proposal. You're willing to negotiate the specifics?"

"Not in the least."

"Then why do you want to know a dissenter's actual reservations?"

"So I may inscribe them on his headstone. We should all be remembered for what we stood for during our brief journeys."

EIGHT

My immediate thoughts were to return to Nocturnat and begin doing some major-league ass kicking. But I realized that would be counterproductive. It would be infinitely preferable to have the Plezrite as friends, if for Mirraya and Slapgren's sake alone. Plus, they would have spirited Sapale into hiding, so my violence would be undirected. Sooner or later, I'd fatigue or make a mistake and they'd get an opportunity to do me in. No, I had to speak with Cala.

I materialized where I had before and ran to her house. I reached up to knock, but she opened the door before I could.

"My what an unpleasant ..." she began to say.

"Can it, Cala. No time for snark. We have a major crisis to solve as soon as possible."

"Very well, come in, why don't you?" she said after I'd brushed past her.

"Are the kids here?"

"Neither the kids nor the parents are. They are in their residence. Shall I summon them?"

I ran my fingers though my hair. "No, just as well they aren't. A lot of what happens next will be your call. You can tell them whatever you like, even if it's short of the whole truth."

"Goodness, I may collapse from shock. You deferring to me where they're concerned?"

"Look, sit." I pointed to the kitchen table. I paced back and forth while she did, then I joined her.

50

"May I offer you some refreshments?"

"No. This is important."

"Then I suggest you begin your tale."

"Sapale and I were evacuating her people to a safe planet when we discovered a planet trying to hide itself."

"Sapale was your mate?"

"*Is*. That's not important now."

"And let me guess. You found a society powerful enough to conceal itself, respected their implied wishes, and left them alone?"

I just glowered at her.

"Sorry. That was not helpful or supportive. You and I think differently, that's all."

"The Plezrite are doing the planet hiding."

Picture me swinging a two-by-four length of lumber and striking Cala squarely in the forehead. That would have had less impact than that word: *Plezrite*. I let her stew over it for a while.

"I assume from your reaction that you know who they are?"

"Yes, I do." She looked at me with wonder, an awe I would never have expected she'd harbor toward me. "Jon Ryan, you are a truly remarkable force of nature. That you found the Plezrite in and of itself would define your life as charmed. Combined with all your other impossibilities, I am struck dumb."

I'd have loved to hit her with a comeback, but I wasn't in the mood. "They kidnapped Sapale as we tried to flee."

"That is a challenging development."

"Tell me about it. What can you tell me about these asswipes?"

"That is a long and complex story, my friend." She took a few deep breaths. "Long ago, we were one race. We were all Deft."

"Were you around then?"

She giggled, despite her generally dour nature. "No. I'm not *that* old. That was hundreds of thousands of years ago."

"But you know about them?"

"Yes, of course. You've seen all my books, right?"

"The one I spoke with had never heard of the Deft."

She rolled her head. "Not very surprising. They were minimalists. Not having books would be consistent with their mindset."

"Which is?"

"They reject complexity."

"She said they rejected your *religious cult inside the world of magic.*"

"I have my version, they have theirs. They are but different views of the same set of circumstances."

"You mean one or both of you are revisionist historians."

"As I said, two varying accounts of one matter. So, you only met one of them?"

"Yes, a platinum hollon a bit smaller than you."

She cringed. "Jon, when you speak the word hollon aloud, please think of it as interchangeable with whatever vulgarization of the concept of anal intercourse might be in your tongue. It is not a thing to speak plainly of, ever."

"Oh. Sorry."

"Don't be sorry, be sensitive. She is referred to as *visant,* a two-joined Deft."

"You mean a male and a female?"

"*Sensitivity,* Jon. Please strive for it. There are no physiologic rules as to which two individuals may become a visant."

"Oh, *gotcha.*" I wiggled a finger at her as I spoke.

She shook her big head in resignation.

"What was her name?"

"Himanai. Weird, eh? She said the couple chooses a new single name after hol ... joining."

"Thank you," she said with genuine relief. "Again, that does not surprise me. They split from us because they wanted other ways, ones they felt were simpler. Wait, you told them about me?"

"No, I didn't. I used the word Deft but didn't discuss you or how few are left."

"That is fortunate. Thank you for your discretion."

"When can we rescue Sapale?"

"Jon, I'm not certain we can. I'm not certain we should even attempt it. It is good you spoke to me without the children. They would have insisted on an assault to free your mate."

"Of course, they would have, I mean *will*. Cala, why are you going to help me?"

"I'm not certain we can take her from them. Jon, they may not have brindas, but they possess powerful magic and are in much greater numbers. How many would you estimate there are?"

"The planet was covered in simple structures. I don't know, but probably millions."

"We four cannot defeat millions."

"We don't have to kill millions of them, just the ones standing between Sapale and us."

"Jon, a world of visants is a dynamic force. Locinar was such a place once. You cannot imagine the flow of power."

"Cala, I'm a simple guy. I live by a set of simple rules. Rule One: you kidnap my brood's-mate, you die swiftly and brutally. My goal is to make the offender's soul full of remorse as I shovel it straight into hell."

"Wow," she said. "I believe you'd do it, too."

"You know I would."

"But in this case, force would be futile."

"Then you'll just have to negotiate Sapale's release. *Then* I'll butcher the ones responsible."

"I can't go to Nocturnat. That would insult them beyond all limits. It would be suicidal."

I pointed outside. "There's a little family genetically and socially isolated from their own kind. If there's a planet full of their kin, they need to be there."

"That is a decision left exclusively to me."

"What decision is *exclusively* yours, Cala?" challenged a quite pregnant Mirraya from the doorway she'd been listening from.

"Hey, look who's here," I chortled.

"Return to your quarters. We will talk of this later," Cala said sternly to Mirri.

"Oh, and then you can give us the Cala-sanitized version of the truth? After you've made all the adult decisions for our *little* heads?" Ooh, the girl was mad.

"This is a matter between this human and me. It is not a public debate. Please respect my authority."

Mirri paced quickly over to the table and plopped into a chair. She folded her hands. "I'm staying."

"Mirraya, this is a very critical point in time. I am explaining my reasoning to your benefactor before he leaves, which will be almost immediately. You are *not* welcome to participate."

"All the more reason for me to stay, then. What's all the hubbub?"

"If you don't tell her, I might have to," I said to Cala. Then Mirri and I stared intently at her, waiting to see how this was going to go.

"You have read about the Plezrite Schism, have you not?"

"Yes. You know that. I also know you two aren't fighting over ancient history.

"Your uncle has found the Plezrite."

"Oh, that is interesting."

"And they kidnapped Sapale as we were running away."

"Then they die, swiftly and brutally."

I gestured toward Mirri. "I told you it was Rule One. The kids know it."

"You wouldn't be banging heads if we were going to race to Sapale's rescue, so I assume you, are reticent to charge in guns blazing. In that case, please watch the children while my mate and I assist our family in an hour of tremendous need." She stood to presumably retrieve the kids and the husband.

"Wait. Sit," commanded Cala. "Let us talk as three adults."

"No," replied Mirri. "We will talk as four adults, or we will not talk."

"I came for a bite to eat, but it looks like I'm getting something a hell of a lot better," said Slapgren from the door. He held the younger child, and the other stood at his side.

"Have a seat," said Cala, "this is now completely out of hand."

"I'll get you some bread and cheese," said Mirri, rising.

"No, just hold this," he said, passing her the baby, "and I'll do it."

The toddler popped up onto mom's lap.

"Now you need to be quiet as a stone, all right? We adults need to talk," I said to the babe.

Jon nodded. I passed him my handheld. He didn't know how to use it, but I signaled Al in my head to show him some cartoon. Instant paralysis.

"What are you three arguing about?" asked Slapgren with a mouth full of food.

"We are not arguing. We are discussing a very serious subject."

"And you two," he pointed to Mirri and me, "don't agree with you." He flipped his hand to Cala.

"Yes," Cala replied.

"Then what are you three arguing about?" he repeated with a big smile.

"Do you recall learning about the Plezrite?" Cala asked him.

He scrunched up his face. "Maybe."

"They were discussed in that four-volume set of red books, the ones with the gold inlay," prompted Mirri.

"Oh yeah, the extra super boring ones. They were rebellious Deft, right?"

"Close enough," said Cala, shaking her head slightly. "Your uncle has located them."

His face beamed. "Cool. When can we meet them?"

"Then they kidnapped his wife," she added.

"Not cool. When do we kill them?"

"You are now up to speed on this discussion. I was telling these two," she pointed at Mirri and me, "we cannot assault a million magical shapeshifters and hope to win."

"Why not? We've got you. And we've got Uncle Jon. And, come to think of it, we've got me."

Mirri punched him.

"The wife, too. Don't forget her."

"Shall we bring the babies into mortal combat or just leave them here to fend for themselves once we're all dead?" asked Cala sourly.

"Good point. I'm back to how could we lose, you, UJ, and me?"

"Oh, so the other brindas stays at home and changes diapers."

"Right," he pointed to Mirri but addressed Cala, "she's on board. It's a done deal."

"We're not attacking a ridiculously superior force," said Cala resolutely. "We are the last Deft. We will not perish as a species."

"But they took uncle Jon's wife. What better reason to defy the odds or die trying?" he asked.

"You may feel that way, but I do not," Cala huffed.

"Okay, you watch the kids, and the rest of us will go."

Cala turned to me and basically whined. "You see the trouble you bring with you every visit?"

"I'm sorry your cousins stole my wife," I snapped.

"You should not have meddled. They clearly wished to be left alone."

"Whether UJ should or should not have contacted them, the fact is he did. And they took an inexcusably aggressive step. They will hand Sapale back, or they will pay dearly. Maybe they'll do both," said Mirraya, resolute.

Cala was clearly distraught. She did not want to engage the Plezrite in any way, shape, or form. She also did not want the last of her kind to march glibly off to death.

"Look, Cala and I go. We will *make* them negotiate. We will make them hear reason. You two stay here with your kids," I said.

"I'm not going anywhere," Cala replied heatedly.

"Then I will go alone," I said flatly.

"No, Uncle Jon. You came here for help, and help you will get," said Mirri. Bless her heart.

"Look, Mirri, this is not war. It's only war if you fight a battle you might win. This is personal. You and Slapgren have a family to worry about. Mine is being held captive."

"Uncle, I know why you contacted the Plezrite," said Mirri, eying me steadily. "You wanted to ensure our family had a chance to live with our own kind. You wanted our children to grow up in a diverse society, to choose the mates of their desire. You didn't go there for laughs and giggles."

"Lord, you do sound a lot like me," I said with a grin.

"You know this, too, Cala," Mirri said harshly. "He did this for us. We will help him fix this."

"Good intentions do not pave a good path. There is much at stake. Everything, in fact."

"We three are Deft," began Mirraya. "We may be the last of the Deft, but I'd also like to think we're the *best* of our people. If we can't help someone who risked his life to help us, then I, for one, don't think we're a species that needs preserving."

"Well said, my love," responded Slapgren. "I could not agree more." He reached across the table to take her hand.

Cala sat silently for several minutes. Then she turned to me. "They'll need a ship."

"Who will?" I asked.

"These adults and their children. When you and I are killed by the damn Plezrite, I don't want them stuck on this rock forever."

I smiled. "I know just who to call. She's human, she's has a fast ship, and she owes me a big favor."

"Why does she owe you a favor, Uncle?" asked Slapgren.

I leaned my head to the other two. "Not with the women-folk around. I'll tell you later." I winked, of course.

Someone, quite possibly *two* people, threw a large chunk of cheese at my head.

NINE

"So, Harhoff, I think you're getting full of yourself," Ardile remarked at mess on evening. They were old friends.

"How so? I'm a humble servant of His Imperial Lord," he replied, patting himself on the chest. "Tell me quickly how I stand out, and I'll remedy the flaw before more take note of it."

Others at the table chuckled.

"First, you are the youngest to be security chief of a vessel this size, and now you have a Descore to satisfy your every whim. Tell me, do you wipe your own ass nowadays?"

"Yes, in fact, I do. Are you volunteering to help, Ardy?"

This time, the others laughed heartily.

"No, I think … er, what's that fellow's name again?"

"I trust you are referring to Jangir."

"Yes," he pointed energetically, "that's it. I think Jangir would be insulted if I tried to step ahead of him in that line."

More chuckles.

"I'll check with him, as you seem to be insistent."

The others were back to bawdy giggles.

"I mean, really, the goon is so energetic, so hard working for a Descore. It's hard to believe he was born to servitude."

"If a job is worth doing, it's worth doing well," replied Harhoff confidently.

"And I trust your rump is spotless," returned Ardile.

The joke had apparently died, since that brought nothing more from the crowd than soft grunts.

"I am glad Harhie here has gone to the trouble and expense to obtain a Descore," said Gardov, pointing his fork. "Lending him to me saves me the burden of so many chores."

"Hear, hear," said another, raising his glass. "To fewer chores and more sleeping."

"Really, you slackers. I was hoping you could devote more time to *work* if I let you borrow my manservant. To think, you piss away your newly gotten time sleeping. Well, I can tell you I'm shocked."

"Do tell. The bags under your eyes seem to have faded nicely since Jangir showed up," responded Gardov.

The group was back to pleasant chuckles at that slight.

"Do you know he was actually able to help organize my personal files?" Medilip nodded grandiosely. "Yes, I couldn't believe a Descore would be so well educated to understand systemization and computer protocol so thoroughly. It's *amazing* what they must learn in their schools these days. I should have thought it was nothing more than how to fold napkins and be generally agreeable."

"Yes, Harhoff, thank you again for your generosity," proclaimed Gardov with another toast. "To the easy life."

They all clinked glasses.

Harhoff knew none of them suspected he was toasting to the abundant intelligence he was gathering with his manservant's aid. It was almost too easy. Then again, these dupes were rather ripe for the picking. Harhoff was doing them a favor.

TEN

As Cala and I climbed aboard *Stingray*, I waved to Mirraya, Slapgren, and their kids. I also waved to Shielan. She'd agreed to stay with the Deft family until our return. If it became obvious we weren't coming back, she would transport them to Vorpace and help get them set up there. She was a good person. If Sapale would have been there, I do believe she would have felt less warmly toward Shielan. That'd be my guess.

One brief bout of nausea later, and we were back on the ground where we'd landed the first time. There was no Himanai or other greeting committee, since we popped into existence without notice. We quickly left the vortex and began walking in the direction Cala suggested, toward a high concentration of houses. She wanted to get some feel for the society before she was forced to confront it. I was in favor of anything that got me closer to retrieving Sapale. To tell the truth, I was itching for a fight. I'm certain Cala sensed that and made a point to assume the lead for this expedition. We both had a lot at stake, but I was the one with the hair-trigger attitude.

After fifteen minutes, a flock of individuals began trailing behind us. A few were visants, but most were typical-looking Deft adults. They held behind us at a respectful distance, just matching our speed. I didn't get any sense of animosity on their part. Neither did I get the impression that they were curious. They were simple keeping an eye on us while waiting to see what we planned on doing. No one was visibly armed.

When we arrived at a large wooded square in the middle of town, Cala stopped, and the pack behind us caught up quickly. They halted twenty-five meters away and remained silent.

Cala turned to them. "We come in peace. We seek the recovery of our shipmate who we believe was detained by your people. Where is she to be found?"

No one answered. No one as much as shuffled their feet nervously. They just watched us.

"I wish to speak to anyone in a position of control. Where will I find that individual?" asked Cala calmly.

Again, there was no reaction from the crowd. The situation was getting creepy. How long would this standoff last?

As we waited a response, a bronze visant landed in front of us. She folded her wings back elegantly and sat back on her haunches. Once settled, she remained as silent as the rest of the observers.

"I am Calfada-Joric. I am a brindas from the planet Locinar. You are my distant cousins. I would speak to you." Then Cala rested back in a identical pose as the bronze dragon.

While the word *brindas* drew no physical response, the tension in the air spiked after she spoke it.

I do believe that if none of the Plezrite spoke, I'd still be standing in the stupid town square looking at two stubborn dragons. Cala was not going to say another peep until someone acknowledged her.

After ten minutes, the bronze beauty spoke. "I am Yisbid, Grand Visionary for this decade."

I had basically no clue what that meant. I guess that didn't matter too much, but I couldn't stop trying to figure out what she did for a living.

"My life is enhanced for knowing you, Yisbid," Cala said formally. She nodded slightly.

"As is mine in turn," replied Yisbid with a similar faint nod.

All right, there were some cultural similarities here. That suggested a good beginning was possible.

"I would know of the reason for your intrusion," said Yisbid formally. That remark wasn't very encouraging.

"I am certain you know it, pfutump. Why do you bother to ask the obvious?" replied Cala. Pfutump was a term roughly equivalent to *little girl*. It wasn't a pejorative, but neither was it a compliment.

"We are unaccustomed to the ways of the brindas. My apologies."

"Common courtesy is not the exclusive purvey of the brindas." Oh yeah, zap.

"Why are you here?"

"The human will recover his mate. She is in the large building down the street on the left-hand side, with the red banner above the door."

Must have been a brindas thing. I couldn't sense Sapale's location.

"She was held to ensure the mate would return. No harm has come to her."

"These things I know. Why is it important the human return if he was not welcome in the first place?"

"Now it is you who ask the painfully obvious."

"It is my way. I am simple. I will simply be treated well, with respect, and my wishes honored."

Man, she was ballsy.

"You do not rule here, witch. Mind your status."

"Pray you never learn of my full status, pfutump. Now, I am old, and I grow weary cackling in the streets with strangers. I will proceed to the building the prisoner is being held and retrieve her."

"She is not a prisoner, and you may not retrieve her."

"She is an honored guest whom you jealously guard because of your fondness for her?"

"She is, as I said, a detainee to ensure the return of the human."

"As he is here, your concerns are at an end."

"You cannot take her by force."

"Is that a statement of *hope* on your part or *ignorance*?"

"Neither. We will not be bullied by heretics."

"Excellent. Neither will I. If you see one, please alert me, and we shall both be rude to them."

"It is unwise to attempt a forceful rescue."

"Then how, child, will I gain the release of my quarry?"

"*If* she is to be released, it can only be through negotiation."

"Hmm. Let us all hope negotiations do the trick, for she *will* be released."

"Come with me. The High Council is prepared to meet with you."

"I seriously doubt that," replied Cala. "Come, Jon Ryan. We go to make nice."

"The human is forbidden to enter the chamber. No alien may attend."

"So, this human's mate, the very subject of my visit, will not be present?"

"Of course, she will. How can they discuss her if she isn't in evidence?"

"And since she is an alien and will attend, so will this odd foreigner. Come, strange beast," she said over her shoulder to me. I liked her style under pressure.

We walked quickly to the building with the red pennant flopping in the breeze. Cala and I followed and entered single file. Our procession ended almost immediately in a large room directly off the foyer. Several visants sat around a round table, along with a few humanoid-formed Deft. Sapale was in a wooden juror's box built into a corner of the room. I waved to her energetically. She shrugged back at me.

"Council members, this is Calfada-Joric. She claims to be a brindas from a planet named Locinar. She has come to request the release of the detainee." Yisbid bowed deeply and withdrew. She closed the double doors as she left.

Immediately, a copper-colored visant spoke. "No one on this council hoped to ever have a member of the arcane religious order present herself to this esteemed body."

"Children often want more than they may receive," Cala said firmly.

"I will ask you to refrain from verbal jousting. This is a very serious matter, and your arrival is even more concerning."

"Will the one doing the asking care to identify herself, or is this to be a secret tribunal?"

"I am Wensist. I sit as council chair this year." Her voice was strained.

"Cousin Wensist, I will stop jousting when you do, not before."

"Are you here to *convert* us, witch?" shouted a humanoid several seats away.

"Not you, for certain, little brain. We heretics *do* have standards."

There was a buzz of chatter around the table.

"Enough. *Silence*," shouted Wensist. "I will ask the members of this council to behave as grown adults, not frightened children. Mancope, please retract your accusation."

Uncertainly at first, the one who called Cala a witch spoke. "I retract my accusation. It was wrong of me to shout it out."

"And not wrong of you to hold it in your mouth?" asked Cala.

"Will the brindas please hold her obviously superior tongue in check?" asked Wensist with obvious frustration.

"As long as it suits my purposes, council chair."

"We assume you are here to beg for the freedom of this alien invader. I must warn you we are disinclined to allow her, or any of you, for that matter, to leave this planet and reveal the secret we have so jealously guarded for so long."

"There is much troubling in your statement, Wensist," Cala began. "First, I have never and will never beg for anything. Second, this alien invader, as you so harshly call her, is no threat to you. Third, do not mistake your inclination to be a force that will affect my personal resolve. Now we can bluster back and forth until dawn, but there is no gain in that. Alternately, we can talk as reasonable souls and accomplish something important."

"What important matters would you have us agree to?"

"Why, the unification of our two societies, naturally."

"You do wish to control our minds, dark witch of hell," shouted Mancope. He stood and pointed at her frantically.

"Will my second please remove that fool from the room?"

A visant rose and placed her talons on Mancope's shoulder. She pushed him forward out of the room. He didn't protest, probably because the talons would have just dug deeper.

"I apologize for his outburst. Mancope is a fine individual, but he fears change. He fears a change involving a religion all the much more," said Wensist.

"I would like to clarify something. I am a brindas. I have studied the mystical ways of all our people, the collective knowledge of our race. I am *not* a priestess, a religious zealot, nor an evangelical of any kind. I am not here to convert you, save your souls, or have you adore me."

"Then why are you here?" asked a visant seated next to Wensist.

"Brother Markum, I believe she has made that clear," interjected Wensist. "She is here to seek reconciliation, reunion."

"I also come to expedite the release of this human's mate." She pointed to me without looking at me.

"I will be honest and forthcoming on that point, Calfada-Joric," began Wensist. "We split from your society a very long time ago for powerful reasons we continue to hold. As the body charged with the preservation of this population, we are challenged to allow anyone knowing of our existence an opportunity to betray our location. If any of you three were to leave, ever, how do we know we could trust you to guard the secret?"

"You have nothing to fear. I can tell you this as a promise," responded Cala. "The human only wanted to confirm your presence so he could alert me. This he has done. I assure you he has no further interest in your world. He will not tell anyone of the Plezrite's position, because he will gain nothing passing such information along."

"And why is it this alien felt it was so important to tell a brindas of our existence? What does he think *you* will gain, *you* will accomplish with that information?" asked Wensist.

"He thinks the last handful of Deft might not die out as a species. That's what he hopes to see come to pass."

That brought mumbling and shuffling all around the table.

"Are you saying there are but a handful of your population remaining? That, before you answer, is difficult to accept or believe," queried Wensist.

"There are five of us left. One is pregnant. Soon we will be six Deft laboring in this sad life. Soon enough, there will be none."

More hushed mumbling circulated.

"Was there a plague? How could all the Deft be eliminated?"

"A conquering force named the Adamant. They murdered all the Deft but us. We numbered in the billions. They came, they slaughtered, and the Deft perished as a race."

"This is beyond tragic and, to be honest, difficult to believe."

"I have the power of zar-not. I offer to join minds with you freely, so you can see the bare truth of it, the stark reality."

Wensist thought a moment. He was clearly stunned. "I will speak for the council. The human female is free to leave, as is the male. We cordially invite you, Calfada-Joric, to remain as our treasured guest. We wish to more fully understand the matter of genocide and the reunification of our people."

"I accept your kind offer." She turned to me. "Go in peace, Jon Ryan. I shall rename you, sir. You are now to be known to the Deft as The Impossible Force. Tell the children I am well and will rejoin them soon. Your kind friend may return home as soon as she desires to."

With that, I helped Sapale jump over the railing of her box, and we walked very quickly to *Stingray*. We were back on Rameeka Blue Green in seconds. I was so relieved. Sapale, not so much. She was so mad at the Plezrite, and she wanted to go back and whoop some butt. Why? Because they called her human. Them were fighting words for my Kaljaxian princess. She was so darn cute it hurt.

ELEVEN

Sapale and I returned by Rameeka Blue Green to bring Mirri and Slapgren up to date. Then we took Shielan home to Vorpace. That way she could leave the ship behind for the Deft to use. She instructed both how to pilot the shuttle, including test flights, so they were comfortable using it. I also wanted to touch base with her big sister to see how the whole mutual defense thing was coming along.

By the way, I was totally blown away by Sapale's reaction to Shielan. In place of instinctive female rivalry, they got along like long lost friends. The two exchanged contact information, drank coffee, laughed together, and made plans to visit each other very soon. I mean, a *little* cat fighting over me might have been nice.

The three of us went right to Jonnaha's office after we landed. "Well look what …" Jonnaha started to say. Then she saw Sapale come in last. "Well, what a surprise," she quickly censored herself.

"I called you not five minutes ago," Shielan said with a puzzled look.

"Yes, you did. I'm surprised it took you so long to get here. I'm dying for coffee, but I wanted to wait until you three got here." She thumbed a button on her desk. "Coffee for four, please." Then she sat back down and smiled like the politician she was.

"Jonnaha this is my wife, Sapale," I introduced.

They shook and exchanged brief pleasantries.

"Your wife. Ah, *newlyweds*?" Jonnaha asked with a squeak.

I looked at Sapale, who looked back at me. "What, two-billion years, give or take?"

She bobbed her head. "Give or take."

Then we both laughed. Shielan knew the whole story, but Jonnaha was compelled to ask, "What? Did I miss something funny?"

"We were only reunited since Jon first came here. He rescued my family from the Adamant conquest of my home world Kaljax," Sapale said with a cordial smile.

"Ah," Jonnaha replied pointing her fingers in opposite directions. "Newly reunited."

"Yeah," I moaned, "before that, she was with a real loser."

Jonnaha was starting to blush. "Who might that be?" she asked uncertainly.

"Me, from an alternate time line."

"Happens every day," observed Shielan.

"So, Jon, it wonderful to see you. I assume things worked out well for your shapeshifter friends since you're all back here so soon."

"The two groups are talking. That's a start," I responded.

"Well, if there's anything else we can do, please don't hesitate to ask."

"Will do. So, how's your glue-together-a-resistance thing going?" I asked.

Her smile disappeared. "It's going, but slower than I would have wished for. Life may be short, but politics are eternal."

"Tell us about it," replied Sapale.

That brought back a smile on Jonnaha's face. "I've browbeaten four additional planets into our loose coalition, so that makes seven so far."

"More prospects on the horizon? I hate to be the one to tell you, but I don't think any less than twenty systems working together will make a difference."

"That's what my military tells me, too. I have so many diplomats out there, it's like a snow storm in space." She seemed thoughtful a second. "We'll see. I *choose* to be optimistic."

"The alternative would be counterproductive," said Sapale.

"Are those cooperating actually cooperating?" I asked.

"Yes. The ones who are in are all in." She chuckled softly. "Those darn

Gorgolinians turned out to be quite industrious." She grinned.

"Those are the fish tank dudes," I said to Sapale.

"They have turned thousands of natural and artificial satellites into mines with nukes. They can be set off manually or by proximity. When the Adamant approach, they're going to have quite the surprise waiting for them."

"Nice," I replied. "Just their planet?"

"No, that's the amazing part. They mined many planets' satellites, even those groups not fully onboard yet. They also scattered booby-trapped debris well out into interstellar space."

"How about the robots?"

"Our partners are far and away the most industrious."

"The robots or the people?" I asked.

"Are you kidding? The robots. The latest craze among the idiotic humanoids is to wear Adamant costumes."

We both guffawed.

"Yes, they're all doing it. When they learned of the imminent invasion, they jumped on that bandwagon. Their theory is that to understand how to defeat the Adamant they need to *be* the Adamant. You know, really get into their heads."

"And if they do get overrun, maybe they'll blend in," I observed with a wicked grin.

"Seriously, I heard someone mention that when I last visited the planet."

"So, the robots are taking matters seriously?" asked Sapale.

"Yes, indeed they are. They came up with a positively frightening war-droid. I've seen holos of its test runs. Impressive firepower and shielding. Those bad boys are going to put a hurt on the Adamant."

"How's production?"

"They're flying off the assembly lines. There are hundreds of thousands of functional units already. If production holds, they promise to export them to all allied worlds after they hit two million units for their own defense."

"When do they estimate that?" I queried.

"Two to three months," she replied.

"That would be *epic*," I responded. "It could be a game changer."

"The best part is that they programmed no self-preservation algorithms into the war-droids. They are equipped with Ais, but they're absolutely fearless."

"Excellent. I might want to get a couple for home defense," I remarked.

"No, we're not having a mindless killing machine in our yard. The neighbors will be upset enough about you already," quipped Sapale.

"What? I'm a great neighbor. They've always *loved* me."

"Need I say anything more than Fourth of July or Christmas?"

"Those are isolated events. Anyway, I'm not that into holidays anymore." She rolled all four eyes. It was cute.

"Can we help in any way?" I asked Jonnaha.

"Sure, but don't you have some deadline or something?"

"I do indeed."

"I'd hate to ruin those plans," she replied.

"I'd hate for them to be ruined, too. Really, I'd be bummed."

"How much longer until whatever ... you know, how long do you have left?"

I sighed. "Just under three months."

"It seems overly generous of you to offer then, I think,"

"Yeah, you're probably right."

"Probably?" shot back Sapale. "No, it is. You've given already and a million times more. No, *now* you work on your Jon Plan, whatever that might be, because you won't tell me what it is."

Somebody was angry with me.

"May we help?" asked Jonnaha.

"I wish you could," I responded, shaking my head. "Oh, how I wish someone could."

TWELVE

"You festering green puddle of puss," seethed EJ, "you think I'm hurting you now? Don't tell me where Sapale is, and I'll crank it up ten notches."

"Si … Sir, there was an invasion. Houses and people were exploding all over the place. I swear I never saw her after she left for the caves with you." Caryp's cousin Nishap-ser was telling the truth. But, as with so many aspects of life, the truth mattered not at all. For one thing, EJ was only partially asking. He was mostly venting.

Nishap-ser was the fifth relative he'd interrogated. Four were now deceased. One was on his way, but EJ had learned nothing except that he had a lot of rage to vent. He wanted to get at the boiling-pot-of-hog-shit Jon "Goodie Two-Shoes" Ryan more than he'd wanted anything in eons. Yes, Sapale would pay dearly for her part in their treachery. But EJ had a special spot in his hatred for the astronaut he'd once been. That abomination would come to an end if it was the last thing EJ ever did. Then he'd kill Sapale. No, he reflected, he'd make the mucus milk shake watch her die, then he'd melt him from the toes up. Wait, wait. He could melt them simultaneously. Yes. They could watch each other literally disappear in agony. Resolution was so reassuring. EJ leaned back against the wall and smiled.

Then he finished off Nishap-ser, who'd begun to whimper most annoyingly.

Pisswad, as he had nicknamed Jon, and Sapale might have gone to ground. That'd make them much harder to find, but not impossible. But he had to think they were off doing good, making the galaxy a better and safer place in which to live and raise a family. The sops couldn't stop being pathetic, even to safe their own hides. EJ had posted a major fortune in reward money for any information as to their whereabouts. So far, a month had passed without a peep. He needed better informants. Competent help was so hard to find.

Where would he go if he were Pisswad? Not Azsuram or Kaljax. No, they were completely under Adamant domination. Earth, as a ruse? No, EJ knew he'd been there recently and would think of that. Oowaoa? Possibly, but EJ had still not discovered where that planet of smug pimples was. He did decide to double his standing reward for information on that rat trap. Even if the pair of traitorous cowards weren't there, it would be gratifying to vent on the pompous Deavoriath. There existed no punishment they did not deserve. He'd be doing God's work.

Was it possible, even conceivable, that Pisswad was in cahoots with the Adamant? If he was hiding amongst them, EJ would never be able to touch an artificial hair on his head. In the million years he'd seen the pissy mongrels rise to power, he'd almost never been able to recruit, bribe, or turn an Adamant. Self-righteous pieces of dog shit. The closest he ever came were those two Midriack guards on *Excess of Nothing,* but one dumbass had gone and gotten himself killed by his own clan leader for some reason EJ could never pin down. Then the other clammed up like the proverbial sphinx. Oh, how he hated every single living creature in the universe. And two non-living robots even more than all the rest combined.

"What do you think?" he asked Nishap-ser's corpse. "Should I interview a few more relatives or try another approach while my dignity's still intact?"

He received no response.

"My thinking exactly. I'll shake down a few of my slimy information merchants instead and see if I can't catch a break." To no verbal prompting, he responded, "Why? Hell, because I feel lucky, that's why."

Nishap-ser continued to say nothing.

"Look, I hate to kill and run, but …" EJ paused and cocked an ear to his victim. "That's great, I'm glad you understand. You, too, pal."

THIRTEEN

Sapale and I were lounging in bed after another make-up-for-lost-time session. Talk about warm glow. She lifted her head and set it on my chest. "You know you're going to tell me, so come on. What are you planning to do to get out of your debt?"

I propped up on my elbows. Looking straight down at her, I gave her a kiss. "It's not that I don't trust you, and it's not that I don't value your input. Do you believe me on that much?"

Reluctantly she pouted and replied, "Yes, I do." She propped up on her elbows and looked at me very intently. "Then why can't you tell me?"

"There's only one possible way I see me coming out of this in one piece. It involves a critical twist." I hesitated. "Dearest love, you know EJ is out there and hunting for us like a pair of golden geese. He's good, damn good."

"Tell me about it."

"He might capture you, which, as much as I hate to say it or think it, is a possibility."

"Then he might torture me and find out your plan. But why would he suspect you had a plan in the first place?"

"He doesn't, but he definitely knows I want to take him out. The "plan" he'd want to know about would be mine for that purpose."

"And if he got that information out of me …"

"He'd screw up my plan, and I'll have to take the fall I agreed to."

"Well, I'll just ask that you tell me as soon as you can, all right?"

"My word of honor," I said crossing where my heart wasn't.

She gave me a peck on the cheek and bounded out of bed.

"You're still miffed at me, aren't you?" I asked.

"Only a little." She smiled back at me. "If it were this much more," she pinched her fingers almost closed, "I wouldn't be doing this."

She flung herself into my arms, knocking me back on the pillows.

I raised my hands and clapped. The lights went off.

In the mess later, we were drinking coffee and silently enjoying the good life. "When it's over, my debt that is, what do you want to do?" I asked her.

"You mean *after* you suffer for all eternity?" She gave me a precious crooked smile.

"Will you wait for me, candle in the window and all?"

"Yes, as long as a chastity belt isn't required, too."

I popped air in my cheek and quickly twitched my head. "I don't know if I can sign off on that clause. My people will get back to your people, okay?"

"So, what do I want to do, *assuming* you are free to do it with me three months from now?"

"Yeah."

"List off the options, and I'll tell you which I like the most."

"That sort of violates the what do *you* want to do part of my query."

"Silly human. I don't care what I do as long as it's with you."

"Aw shucks, talk about putting me on the spot." I looked away, embarrassed.

"You know quite well what we'll be doing. We'll be fighting the Adamant like demons from hell."

"Did you have to use that analogy?"

She looked up, replaying her remark in her head. "Oops. Bad taste, right?"

"Anyway, you were saying?"

"Whatever the outcome of the battle along the frontier, the Adamant will still be everywhere . Your goal has been to destabilize them with a death blow. But it will take a very long time for that death to come. You and I will do everything in our power to hasten their demise, but it will be a long and hard struggle."

"It's looking that way."

"Has your contact amongst the Adamant given you any feedback lately?"

"Nah, nothing. Last time he secreted me a report, it sounded like same old same old. He *is* encouraged by the rebellious murmurs he hears. But there are no sustained changes or shifts."

"Do you think his approach is valid?"

I rocked my head. "Maybe. I had the Als run a ton of sims. Most support the notion that an unstable empire will implode due to pent up forces. The personal quests for power and the usual political dissent that any large group spawns seem to make it inevitable."

"So, we fight for the good cause."

"Again."

She started to giggle. "And again, and again."

"You'd think two grown people would learn, right?"

"Hey, who you calling people? I'm not a person. I'm a Kaljaxian alpha-bitch."

"You want'a fight about that?"

She set her mug down gently. "Why yes, I believe I do."

I clapped my hands.

She clapped hers.

FOURTEEN

Garustfulous, or rather Jangir, sat in the dark room hunched over the display screen. The yellow-green computer light made his grin of self-satisfaction look as twisted and convoluted as his feelings were at that moment. He had used Naford's retinal pattern to unlock all the files the third officer of the vessel could access. Those were most of the tactical and many of the secure political files the ship was privy to. Jangir was a naughty kid in a candy shop of espionage. Unfortunately, he'd had to separate Naford's head from his body to do so, but that was now Harhoff's problem, not his. Their working agreement was that the amoral Jangir would collect intel. The only slightly principled Harhoff would cover tracks and forward the information. He'd never been called upon to cover such glaring, bloody tracks before. Jangir really liked that part of his act.

He had a visual recorder copy everything he viewed. He didn't want to plug in an electric component because such an action might be detected. Someone would correctly suspect that what happened actually did take place. Jangir prided himself on being …

What? This had to be incorrect. He scrolled up and read back down. He skipped to the bottom to see who signed the order. Spirits and Forces, it was Lesset himself. This was bad. This was *very* bad. Jangir made a second image of the entire document and shut the system down. He leaned back in the chair and breathed out heavily. Ticks and worms, he thought. This changed everything.

FIFTEEN

"Jon, as wonderful as it is to see you again, really, it's hardly been a couple weeks," said Jonnaha with a puzzled look on her face. "Ah, may I offer you coffee or tea?"

"Both," I said. "Strong and lots of them. It's going to be a late night."

She glanced at her wrist watch. "Jon, it's only ten in the morning."

"I know."

"This sounds bad," she responded.

"It is not bad," replied Sapale.

"Oh good. You had me scared for a mom—"

"It's much worse than bad. *Completely* worse," I tossed in.

She slumped just a little in her chair, then stiffened. "I'll summon my key personnel. They'll be here in less than twenty minutes."

I shook my head. "Make it ten. This is epic."

Within fifteen minutes, all her heads of department and confidential advisors were in the Ready Room around a massive table. The air was tense. It was going to get a whole lot worse once I started talking. I really wished this wasn't coming down. No one in this room, no one in this galactic sector, deserved the news I was about to drop on them.

"We're all here, General Ryan. Why don't you begin?" Jonnaha said formally and with foreboding.

"Thank you. I have received a report that the Adamant are advancing their timeline for attacking this sector. This region *was* in the five-to-ten-year zone.

It has been reprioritized. It has just been moved to the top of the list. It is the *next* area to be assimilated." I let the gravity of that sink in a bit. "Whereas you had years to prepare before, you now have weeks. Maybe they will delay a few months if you're extremely lucky. My intelligence is deficient on this aspect. But you will be attacked with the full might of the empire very shortly." I sat back down.

The room was as quiet as a long-abandoned mausoleum. No one as much as shifted nervously in their chair or reached for a drink of water.

Finally, Jonnaha spoke, though hesitantly at first. "Are you confident the intelligence is reliable and correct?"

I sighed. "Yes. One hundred percent."

"Not that it truly matters, General Ryan, but do you know why the Adamant moved us to the top of the list?" asked a man two seats to Jonnaha's right wearing a military uniform with a ton of fruit salad on his chest.

"Yes, I do. They either have excellent intelligence services of their own, or they have a network of spies. Somehow they became aware of your attempts to put up a unified defense and felt it was prudent to deny you that opportunity."

There was profound silence again.

The same man spoke. "Wasn't it *your* idea to ally ourselves against the Adamant's future assault?"

"Admiral Halkins, I will not tolerate that remark or it's incendiary implications. You will *apologize* to General Ryan immediately and *formally* withdraw that insult." Man-o-man, Jonnaha was hot.

"It was a legitimate military question," he defended. "We need to understand exactly what it is we face and know precisely who our enemy is."

Shielan rose. As coolly as an ice cube in an igloo she stated, "Madame Prime Minister, permission to shoot Admiral Halkins here and now." She slipped her hand inside her jacket where her pistol was holstered.

Jonnaha waved her palm down. "Denied. We are all here for the same reason. If we can't speak our minds, we really stand no chance of success. Admiral, I am still waiting for your apology." The look she gave him. Wow, it was impressive.

"I don't need an apology," I said. "The dude spoke out of fear and ignorance. Times as they are, it's perfectly understandable that an armchair warrior would get jumpy."

Halkins started to rise, then thought better of it. He'd insulted me, and I'd insulted him back. We were enemies, and it was a draw.

Jonnaha shook her head slowly, and Shielan snickered a bit too loudly.

"If you insist. Moving on, are there any *other* questions?"

"I have one. General Franklin Pierce here, commander of joint planetary forces. Do you have any idea what formation the enemy will use or which solar systems will be targeted first?"

"No, but I have a lot of experience fighting them. I believe they will attack all targets simultaneously with immense force."

"But, even if they only target the systems with formal mutual defense commitments, that would be twelve different solar systems spanning nearly four parsecs. If they mean to take the entire five-to-ten-year zone at once, their numbers would have to be unimaginable."

"And they are. Look, the Adamant are like the sand on a big beach. They are uncountably numerous and value each other's lives as much as those grains of sand do. There's a very good reason they've been as successful as they have been."

"Is there a winning strategy?" asked a suit to Jonnaha's immediate left.

"I do not know."

"What can we do?" he asked, clearly near tears.

"Fight. That's all anyone can ever do. You have had a few months to prepare that you wouldn't have had otherwise. That's a plus. The war-droids of Langir will now be a real factor in this fight. But you fight. The alternatives are to run or to lie down and wait for the juggernaut to grind you into the dirt."

"Is flight an option?" someone called out.

"No, of course it is not," shouted Jonnaha. "Come on, people, let's keep our heads attached for a little while longer, shall we?"

"But ... but I mean if General Ryan had a secret plan to move Sotovir or transport its pop—"

"He does not. If you grasp at one more imaginary straw, Phelps, I'll have you thrown out of the room. Is that clear? I value the input of the Department of Food Integrity, but I will not have you derail our planning."

"Yes, ma'am," he whimpered. I hoped that idiot wasn't called upon to aid in the defense of the civilization. He'd cause a mess when he lost bowel and bladder control when the first Adamant rose above the horizon.

"So, they're coming soon, they're coming in devastating numbers, and we're as prepared as we're going to be. That about sum it up, Jon?" asked Jonnaha.

"Yes."

"Do you have any specific thoughts, recommendations, or prayers to offer?"

"Not just now."

"Then I thank you, Sapale, and your spies for giving us as much notice as possible. You're welcome to remain, or you may go. Naturally we would appreciate your extensive familiarity with our foe as we plan."

"We will stay," replied Sapale. "We want to help as much as possible. Plus, I personally would not like to turn my back on that pig but keep him where I can see him." Yeah, she pointed at Admiral Fart Cloud. Nice. You-know-who snickered again.

The meeting dragged on for twelve hours. A few potty breaks were the only respites. Food was brought in and eaten while working. The diplomats of many other systems joined in at odd intervals. It was controlled chaos, at best. The bare bones of a mutual plan were outlined and tentatively agreed upon, pending each government's review. That meant we all did a lot of work that would only possibly be adopted. But it was a start. It also served to formally light as big a fire as there was ever going to be under everyone's collective backsides. It was go time, and at least that message was loud, clear, and undeniable.

I only wished they stood the remotest chance of success. But I knew better.

SIXTEEN

The Lead Point Room was packed. High Wedge Lesset, Prime of the Secure Council, sat at the middle of a long metal table. He was flanked by the other eleven members of the council. Their raised stage gave them an excellent perspective of the Supreme Directive Wall off to their right. They also had a full view of the auditorium seats that ascended to the left. All one hundred and fifty seats were taken by senior command officers. Hushed chatter produced a charge of palpable excitement in the air. This was what the Adamant lived for. Conquest, domination, and the disbursement of death.

"All right, come to order. We have much to do and much more to accomplish," announced Vice Prime of the council Kemflode.

The room instantly fell silent.

Lesset rose to his full height and rested his arms on a short podium. "Fellow leaders of the Adamant Empire, welcome to our last meeting before we begin the assimilation of twelve new systems. Glory be to His Imperial Lord Palawent."

The crowd roared back a cheer for the emperor, who never attended these important meetings. It had been discovered many years before that when the emperors did attend, they mistakenly thought they were in charge and that their opinions mattered. Such distractions were no longer welcomed or tolerated.

"As you know, our last campaign was perfectly successful. We destroyed the militaries of six worlds in five systems in one fell swoop."

Another cheer rose up, this time for Lesset.

"Those missions are now in their mop-up phases. We are now free to proceed to the next obstacles to our domination. As you know, the emperor, in his infinite wisdom, has instructed us to skip over a few minor pockets of resistance. He has foreseen a growing threat in the Gamma-Epsilon Sector, near the galactic edge. Our new mission is to extinguish that threat before it may be allowed to become significant. All praise be to Emperor Palawent."

A lesser cheer rose up in response. Almost no one in the room gave a ragged chew toy for the imperial waste of space.

"I have given individual orders to the Wholes who will lead our attack. Wedge Leaders will receive their assignments from their specific Wholes immediately following this assembly. Our conquest will begin in two days at Standard Dawn, as usual. I will expect all victories to be accomplished in less than *three* days on *all* fronts on *all* planets."

That brought a rush of murmurs from the crowd. Three days was an unusually short time to crush an entire planet's resistance. A week was a short time. Three days was unprecedented. It signaled that the Secure Council wanted these planets to suffer mightily. They were to never know what hit them. They were to be an example of the brute and brutal force of the Adamant Empire. The bloodlust that was typically high at these meetings shot to redline. Everyone wanted to lock their jaws on the throats of their enemies.

"I would wish you all luck, but you do not need such a crutch. You are the best warriors, the best commanders, and the best *killers* to ever prowl the galaxy. I would feel sorry for what your victims are about to suffer, but they are beneath us and below our contempt. Now go forth and *kill*. Go forth and *slaughter*. Go forth and drink the blood of those who *insult* the Adamant by existing. Show *no* mercy. Give *no* quarter. Leave *nothing* living in the wake of our tidal wave of *victory*."

Everyone rose and cheered with abandon. All-encompassing death was so glorious. It defined what it was to be happy, to be fulfilled. It defined what it was to be Adamant.

SEVENTEEN

"Cala, we understand your position. Truly, we *hear* you. But you must understand this issue from the Plezrite point of view." Yisbid struggled to conceal her growing frustration. "This touches on the very reason we used our collective magic to remove our solar system from the galaxy. We wish not only to be left *alone,* but we wish to be *unburdened* by galactic politics and chicanery."

"But I'm not certain you *have* a choice. Any choice. Yes, as far as any of us know, you're invisible to the Adamant, but that doesn't mean you *are.* Even Jon Ryan, with his unprecedented spy network, can't tell us for certain. You may be fooling yourselves, deluding yourselves into not only a false sense of having no moral obligation to help the rest of us, but a false sense of security."

"Mistress Cala, we have discussed those very issues in our councils, as you well know. *We,* as Yisbid just stated, have heard your requests and warnings. But the results of our debates have been insufficient to change our fundamental philosophy. We want to continue being who we are and go along doing what we have for a very long time," said Himanai with thinly veiled contempt.

"Translation: *your* problems are not *our* problems," Cala hissed back angrily.

"I am very sorry you see it that way," responded Yisbid. "I feel your pain. I wish reality was different than it is, but it is not. We are, for the last time, unable to help you fight the Adamant. You and your students are welcome to move here and become valued members of our society, of our culture. But we will not offer you military aid."

Cala rested back on her haunches, in a defensive stance. "You use interesting words, Yisbid. Do you fully hear them?"

"I know what I said. Please point out where you think I might be enlightened."

"Prescient, indeed, are your thoughts."

"Are you baiting us or playing a riddle game to insult us?" Himanai asked sharply.

"I speak now only to the Grand Visionary, not the rabid cow."

"Well, I—" Himanai spat out as she stood.

"Sit," instructed Yisbid, setting a hand on her arm to restrain her. "I am listening, Cala."

"Do you know why your title is Grand Visionary? I'm fairly certain you do not."

"I am the leader of the Plezrite for a ten-year period this cycle. That individual is called the Grand Visionary." She spoke cautiously, knowing there was some trapdoor awaiting her.

"*Bah*. You don't. The office of Grand Visionary is ancient. It was in place when our two people were still one. Back then, it indicated which Deft brindas was responsible for using the Vision."

"I've never heard of this nonsense," Himanai said through clenched teeth.

"No. Cows, rabid or otherwise, need only chew cud and fart."

"Cala, please excuse my assistant. She is young and does not honor you as she should. Please proceed," responded Yisbid.

"The Vision is a thing. It is a power. The Grand Visionary was charged with using it for the benefit of the community."

"You make it sound dangerous," she replied.

"Oh, it is not. But the *knowledge* it brings, that can be more dangerous than a poisoned knife at your throat."

"What is the Grand Visionary supposed to see that I'm unaware of?"

"The future, child. Your job is to see the future on behalf of your people."

"That doesn't sound very dangerous, you old witch," shot back Himanai.

Yisbid spun on her. "Leave this instant, rotten one." Once Himanai had reluctantly skulked out of the room, Yisbid continued. "I clearly do not see into the future."

"But *I* do," replied Cala.

Yisbid stiffened. "What is your point?"

"As Grand Visionary, I would show you the future. It would then be yours to judge whether the Plezrite chose wisely or chose poorly today."

"That's utter nonsense," replied Yisbid with obvious uncertainty.

"How so, child?"

"You will place some image in my mind that affirms your contention. The future is not ours to know."

"Spoken by the non-brindas in the room. As to placing a favorable image in your mind, I can assure you I will not. That, by the way, is a trivial thing to do. I can do it without The Vision. Here, I feel a demonstration is in order. What is your favorite dessert?"

"Arch-fudge. Why?"

"And where would you love to eat it? What special place if you had your choice of all locations?"

"My mate's arms. Again, I ask ..."

Yisbid fell mute. Her eyes glazed over, and her breath began to become labored. Then she gasped and jerked her head backward.

"Ho ... how did you do that?" she challenged.

"By the powers controlled by a brindas. Wasn't the candy delectable?"

Yisbid sat silent a moment. "Yes, better than any I've ever had."

"So, now you know that if I wanted to place an image in your mind, I could at any time. I will escort you to a vision of the future if you are brave enough to see it."

Again, she reflected a few seconds. "Very well. I do not want to make a mistake I would come to regret. How dangerous is this journey?"

"It depends on the traveler. One who is strong, fearless, and knows herself is generally safe."

"And what of lesser mortals?"

"They go stark-raving mad when they see the future."

"When may we begin?"

"Come stand by my side, and we shall sally forth."

Yisbid came around the table and stood next to Cala. The brindas took her companion's hand. "Close your eyes and clear your mind."

"How long will—"

Yisbid did not finish the question. Their minds were no longer locked in the present.

Seconds later Yisbid gasped like she was drowning. Cala opened her eyes and relaxed her body, seemingly unaffected by whatever had just transpired. Yisbid crumpled to her knees and covered her face forcefully with both hands. She began to softly wail.

Someone rushed to her side. "Yisbid, are you all right? Can I help? You there," she called out to a couple male bystanders, "come help me get her to the doctor."

The men rushed forward. They each grabbed under a shoulder and tugged at the Grand Visionary.

Yisbid shot to her feet and shook her would-be helpers off roughly. "I'm fine. Release me."

Everyone backed away slightly.

Yisbid turned to Cala. "Did you see what I saw?"

"I was there also. I saw everything."

"But how?"

"What did you see, Yisbid?" asked someone close.

"I saw our planet. It was on fire."

"But then you didn't see the future, only a vision. No planet, Nocturnat included, can be engulfed in flames. There is no air in space to sustain such a blaze."

"It was on fire, but not with a natural one. The flames were of our own making."

"No," screamed another person. "Why would we set fire to our own world?"

"To kill the Adamant who defiled Nocturnat's sacred soil. They had vanquished the Plezrite. We chose mutual death over servitude."

"No," the man gasped softly. "When?"

Cala finished the thought for Yisbid. "Very *soon*, child."

EIGHTEEN

I was on Sotovir when the all-out Adamant assault began. It was just thirteen days after I broke the news to the leaders of Vorpace. Right about when I expected it. I'd fought countless wars in every imaginable setting. I'd struggled against the Adamant personally for a couple years. Still, I was overwhelmed and awestruck with their battle plan. It was truly impressive.

Adamant warships of every imaginable size and kind simultaneously popped up over Sotovir and eleven other planets. Some were specialized in planetary bombardment. Those were massive. Others were smaller, yet still huge, and designed to fight ship to ship in space, defending against any aerial responses. Still others were stripped down troop carriers with little more than standing room for millions upon millions of ground assault personnel.

I watched from the safety of *Stingray,* perched on a hill, with a partial membrane up. Their initial action was to begin raining fire from above. So many plasma bolts and metal balls were dropped that the entire atmosphere flashed into a brilliant waterfall of death and destruction. The ground rose up in anguish, hurled itself into the sky only to be pounded back down by the relentless onslaught from above. That softening up lasted fifteen minutes. The damage caused was stunning, and I was on Sotovir. It was the planet best suited to weathering such a withering attack. The fish-tank Gorgolinians had little construction on the surface since their lives were spent underground or in caves. As a result, the Adamant explosions caused much less damage than on, say, the human world of Vorpace. But less was only relative. Gigantic craters and smoking ruins were everywhere.

The moment the bombardment ceased, I saw the landing craft drop from the sky. It turned to twilight there were so many. Within a couple minutes, the hatches burst open and Adamant gushed out, as if shot from a water cannon. With their legendary organization and discipline, they moved quickly into ranks and advanced to their assigned targets. If it wasn't so horrific, it would have been marvelous to witness.

Then the Gorgolinians counterattacked. They sprang from the ground like crabs on a beach. They pulled countless Adamant down holes, never to emerge again. The fish tanks proved to be a hell of a lot tougher than I would have guessed. Salvoes of plasma bolts hit them, but they kept firing and seizing Adamant. Once they had a dog in their clutches, he was a goner. The Gorgolinians had scissor-shaped claws that snipped their foes in half like they were paper dolls. With their hard shells, they didn't favor taking cover, so they advanced rapidly into the Adamant ranks.

For just a moment, I thought their physical advantages might swing the battle. But that moment passed soon enough. Slowly, the Gorgolinians fell or were blown up. The Adamant had figured out several of their weaknesses and exploited them with a vengeance. In only a few minutes, there were few fish tanks left standing, as far as I could see.

The Adamant units regrouped and ran toward their original targets. That's when a second wave of Gorgolinians sprang from the ground like a farmer's worst nightmare. They hit the Adamant from behind, totally by surprise. Though the canovir buckled, they did not panic. With their engrained discipline, they rallied and pushed their attackers back. Another swarm of Gorgolinians then rose at the backs of the turned Adamant. They tried a pincer maneuver to force them into hand-to-hand combat. They figured that in close quarters the enemy would be less able to use their blasters.

Slowly, the locals gained an upper hand. Finally, I couldn't make out sharp ranks. The combatants were blended in chaos. It was like a blender with living beings tossed in by the bucketful. I think if that battle ended then, the Gorgolinians would have won. But more and more landing crafts deposited endless reinforcements. The whirling combat ended when the recently arrived

Adamant began firing indiscriminately into the melee, killing friend and foe with equal ferocity. Within a few minutes, nothing moved in the combat zone. With grim intensity, the ring of Adamant reinforcements closed to the center of the circle, shooting anyone still alive on either side. Their tactic obviated the need to medically evacuate their own troops. That would have distracted from the primary mission, which wasn't to win with minimal casualties. No, it was to win, period.

In less than an hour, the fighting was over. Tens of thousands of Adamant advanced to sweep areas of habitation. Others labored to stack the dead for cremation. Still others began establishing command centers, outhouses, and large mess and dormitory tents.

Pops of plasma fire flared to life occasionally as the unstoppable force advanced. I waited around just long enough for them to have finished occupying most of the structures. Then I blasted them and any occupants into the rewards of the afterlife. Once they identified me and a bombardment began, I folded away, back to Vorpace. In no way did the pittance of damage I did made me feel any better. It certainly made no difference. Damn, the Adamant were good at war. Double damn them.

NINETEEN

I folded back into real space at a predesignated location near the capital. Sapale had remained behind to help coordinate the defense of Vorpace. Unlike with the Gorgolinians, the humans here had two important new weapons. A small number of membrane generators and a few war-droids from Langir. The leaders of Sotovir had refused any such toys, preferring to battle in their traditional manner.

Deploying shield units was very problematic. I didn't have time to prepare many. The bigger issue was that none of them could fall into the Adamant's grimy paws. That technology would be way too powerful in their already indomitable armamentarium of domination. Any I deployed had to be paired with an AI in control of a powerful self-destruct explosive. But, key facilities such as major hospitals and troop aggregations could be protected from the initial bombardment. The handful of war-droids were to be set against the Adamant as soon as they landed with the hope of unnerving them, or at least disrupting their ranks.

When I arrived, the orbital assault had been concluded, and the landing craft had just coughed out the first wave of foot soldiers. The delay stemmed from the greater number of major cities and the presence of the membranes. At first, the Adamant didn't seem to understand why the structures they targeted didn't go boom. Consequently, they addressed prolonged fire at them before they abandoned that approach. Lucky me, I got to see the Adamant victory emerge from brave yet futile resistance all over again.

This time, however, I was not going to be a bystander. Facing eternal torment in the very near future, I was planning on being the local franchise of the Hell On Wheels Death Delivery System. *Oorah*.

"How did it go?" asked Sapale as she rushed to embrace me.

Jonnaha and her cabinet remained where they were, watching the unfolding mayhem.

"Better than I would have guessed," I replied, pulling her in tightly.

She lifted her head from my chest. "You mean they held the Adamant off?" She was totally shocked.

"No. They just died a lot slower and took a lot more dog with them than I anticipated. In the end, it was the massacre we all expected."

I felt her slump in my arms.

"But this time, The Demon of Death Jon Ryan is taking up a personal collection. They don't stand a chance."

"Wow. Where's my handheld when I want a selfie with the legend before his next miracle? Photo's gonna be valuable after you single-handedly slay *that* beast."

I kissed her forehead. "Showtime." We parted, and I stepped over to Jonnaha. "How's it looking?

"Grim. Jon I never thought I'd watch my combined armed forces march off to certain death. I hate the feeling. I *hate* the Adamant."

"You're welcome to step in line behind me. Look, you didn't ask for this. They forced it on you. Your job is to make them pay as dearly as possible. That's all any of us can do."

I heard a metallic squeak and looked to find the source. It was one of the pair of war-droids positioned against the far wall in the room. It must have sneezed. They were placed here in reserve, anticipating the worst. That's when I noticed Shielan. Gone was her silk suit. She was in full army regalia from flak jacket to spit-polished boots. She sported twin plasma rifles and a look on her face that could kill.

"Hey kid," I said to her, kissing her Kevlar helmet, "you look different. Have you lost weight or what?"

She winked. "No, I just copied the pinup I had of you in my bedroom.

I'm a killing machine like my hero. *Surar*."

"Okay, nice, but you gotta get it right. Repeat after me. It's *oorah*, not *surar*."

"Do you have somewhere to go and die?" she asked.

"Yes. Why?"

"Then I suggest you go there so I don't feel the need to kill you here, sir."

I gave her a salute and walked back to Sapale. "I'm leaving the vortex. When the time comes, use it to evacuate as many as you can." I turned and pointed at Shielan. "Just don't bring her. She smells funny."

"No, no, and no. That wasn't the plan. You take the cube. There are several ships here if we need to evacuate."

"You know what the best part of being the general in charge of a military operation is? Go on, take a wild guess."

"Someone else cuts your meat for you at dinner?" she replied with a puzzled look.

"No, but that's nice, too. No, the best part is during that all too brief period you can tell your wife what to do."

She started to say something but relaxed back into silence.

"There's my girl," I said, tapping her cute little nose. "Honey, if I mosey down the hill or fly to the far side of the planet, it doesn't matter. I'm going to be killing Adamant, and they're probably going to kill me back. Location isn't that important." I smiled. "Your safety, however, is."

"I love you," she said to my face.

"Crap, I was just about to say that. You stole my thunder."

"Jon."

"Yes."

"Please leave now."

"Sure thing."

I jogged out the door. A small squad of soldiers fell in behind me, and we rattled out the door and down the hill. The membrane pulsed to allow us though and then zapped back into existence as soon as the last woman was past. I could immediately smell the meat-locker in the air. War. The same old same old.

Our path led to the outskirts of the capital city. It was currently free of the Adamant horde, but the sound of intense firefight was not far off. We advanced in the open, covered by my personal membrane. Our weapons were set on visual frequencies, so we could fire though the shield. I had to hope the Adamant hadn't accounted for that yet and would be using standard plasma guns. Straggling refugees moved past us as quickly as they could, but at that point, any sane person had left the city for the established shelters in the country. We couldn't stop to offer help. Our mission was strictly offensive, not humanitarian.

First contact came quickly. We rounded a corner, and a huge tank was on top of us. It fired three quick plasma blasts. It waited for the dust to clear to verify we were little cinders. By the time they could see my squad, we had scrambled halfway up the vehicle. Several detonators were magnetically clipped on, and we vaulted off. As we ran for cover in a building, a plasma bolt slammed into the membrane, and the tank erupted in flames.

One of my team started to cheer, but I stared him down quickly. He got the message. Celebrate if we win. Otherwise keep fighting.

Backup foot units converged on us from three sides. We started shooting. A few Adamant face-planted from their full sprint. Others fanned out and took cover. It took them a few minutes, but then they began bypassing the membrane with handguns adjusted to the correct frequency.

"They're onto us," I shouted into my headset. "Dropping the membrane *now*. Switch to plasma weapons and spread out some. Everyone stay with the squad and watch our flanks."

The others moved a few meters away and hunkered down. Once the enemy noted our weapons had changed, they knew the shield was down. Hundreds flooded the street and charged with a deafening howl. My team laid down a torrent of plasma, but the fallen dogs were crushed to the asphalt by the advancing wave slamming over their corpses.

They'd trained on this suicidal attack. Crazy sonsabitches. I swept my finger laser at knee height and each advancing row of dogs toppled in agony. But still they came. We began falling back rapidly, keeping up our fire the entire time. We barely kept pace. I tossed three thermite grenades to the front, middle, and rear of the onslaught.

Boom.

Boom.

Boom.

Bodies arced upward, and those not airborne fell like bowling pins.

In the confusion, I yelled into my headset. "*Run.*"

We sprinted as fast as we could. A few seconds later, the man on my right exploded, and he fell to the ground trailing smoke.

We broke for cover.

The advance was reforming, and a few Adamant knelt and were taking aim.

I hit the dirt and started blistering them with rail shot. I always carried my good old rail rifle into battle. No one expected it, and everyone was unnerved when a depleted uranium ball traveling at eighty percent of the speed of light landed near them, hopefully where their head used to be. I loved the sound of the explosions. They were so definitive.

I missed a dog low. The ground volcanoed up and ripped anyone close to shreds. The Adamant stopped advancing and leapt for cover.

"I need air cover. Sector Fifteen, 11-239 by 44-667," I yelled to the command center.

"Negative, all air units neutralized. Sorry, you're on your own."

"Any artillery? Mortars?"

"I have mortars, conventional and thermite, that can reach your position."

"Conventional thirty meters plus north by northwest of my ping." I pinged our location.

"Roger that. Stand by."

"Like I got a choice. Ryan out."

I commenced firing again. Two others in my squad had bought the farm, and one was nowhere to be seen. Maybe dead, wounded, or running like hell. I sent up a hand signal to drop back. The woman next to me and I laid down covering fire.

The Adamant were advancing doorway to doorway on both sides of the street. I heard at least one tank roaring just around the corner. That's when the mortar rounds started dropping. The explosions were scattered at first, but then the street in front of me erupted in debris and smoke. The tank barely cleared the last building before it exploded. It crashed into a building and stopped, smoke pouring from its underbelly.

I signaled to split into two groups to try and flank behind the Adamant currently pinned down. Three soldiers went left. The woman and I broke right. I sprinted two blocks, then made two left turns to try and come in behind the enemy position. Crap. I miscalculated their number. Instead of coming around their backsides I ran straight into a solid column of grunts.

They fired first. The wall next to my head was pitted with searing holes.

I threw a couple grenades, but that just split the advancing troops without even slowing them.

"*Retreat*," I screamed into my headset.

Just as the woman at my side turned, her right arm vaporized. She spun to the ground screaming and multiple bolts struck her where she lay.

Ten Adamant vaulted over her body and were closing on me. I put up a full membrane. I was in total defensive mode. I knew I was surrounded already. The bastards would never leave until they got through to me. I sat down roughly while slinging my rifles onto a shoulder. What next?

It struck me out of the blue. I could expand the membrane fifteen, maybe twenty meters the way it was configured. I knelt and swung both rifles around, one in either hand. I expanded the membrane symmetrically and jumped to the side nearest the building I was covering in. I opened the membrane in a clam-shell configuration pointing toward where I was had been kneeling and immediately slammed it shut.

I was in the middle of a battered office. Outside, many Adamant lay strewn on the ground. Those behind them looked confused, but then a few saw me and opened fire just as the membrane snapped closed.

I repeated the expansion, moving farther toward the back of the building. I opened the shield like before. This time I saw the entire skyscraper falling away from me like a felled mighty redwood tree. The enemy on the other side of the structure stood zero chance of survival. Fine by me. I scrambled to my feet and ran away from the street where the column of troops had been moving toward my initial position. I was on my own. The others were either dead or permanently separated. I headed in the direction that afforded me maximal cover. As I passed the first building, I took cover and checked my rear. No one was pursuing. Perfect.

Surely the soldiers who'd pinned me down reported a human with a personal membrane device. That meant the big dogs knew I was on the ground. That would draw an instant increase in the numbers. I think by then *Jon Ryan* must have been a swear word in their culture. I elected to circle back to the Command Center where Sapale was. My effectiveness on the ground was severely limited as it stood, and it looked to get much worse quickly.

Halfway back, I hit a major concentration of enemy infantry. They had three tanks and something that looked like a helicopter. I'd never seen one before, so I wasn't sure. I wasn't going *through* that force, so around it had to be. I broke right and stayed low. Moving fast, I made it past the enemy's flank. To avoid contact, I had to swing several blocks clear of them.

Once safely behind them, I made for HQ again. Not a block later, something above and behind me began a strafing run. The sidewalk exploded on either side of me, and I was pelted with rocky shards. As soon as they pulled up because of the tall buildings, I dived into the next doorway and looked up.

There. A hybrid fighter, both space and atmosphere capable. But that meant it was slow and handled poorly. You can't build one small craft that can fly in both places well. I guessed which direction it would reemerge from and pointed both rifles just over the tops of that building. Sure enough, five seconds later it screamed into view, and I opened up. A rail ball struck it amidships, and it split into two fiery halves. They sailed out of view. But I'd betrayed my position. I had to move fast to stay ahead of a whole lotta trouble.

I sprinted down the sidewalk with a partial membrane over me like a beach umbrella. Within a couple blocks, it was being pounded with plasma bolts. I rolled into cover and checked where the shots were coming from. Dude, I almost began laughing. It looked like an AT-AT walker from the ancient classic, *Star Wars*, spindly legs, ungainly gait, and all. Then the sidewalk right in front of me exploded, and I was no longer amused. I aimed my rail gun at a lower joint and blew it out. The upper unit staggered like a drunk ostrich a few seconds then crashed to the side.

I took off again, heading literally for the hills. The pursuit was too hot to hope to move toward HQ. I was running for my life. Anywhere was better than where I was. I made for parts unknown with maximal haste.

Several blocks later, I ran into a small squad of soldiers. I saw them first, but one of them heard me. He signaled the group to fan out and directed them toward the sound. Eight infantrydogs. Okay, I could take them. I dropped to a prone firing position and unshouldered my plasma gun. They were not two meters away when I opened up. Four careened backwards with flaming chests before the others reacted. They hit the deck and returned fire. I rolled to my left and popped up shooting. One lost an ear, one his head. The remaining Adamant pinned me back down.

All is fair in love and war, right? I deployed a partial membrane and shot to my feet with my hands in the air. "I *surrender*. Don't shoot." I yelled. "I surrender."

The three remaining soldiers rose to a crouch, one holding his wounded ear. "Drop your weapon," one shouted back.

I made a show of tossing first one rifle, then the other to the ground. They advanced cautiously.

"Do not move," said the one who'd spoken earlier.

"Wouldn't dream of it," I said in a conversational tone.

"Is it The Dreaded One?" asked the soldier pressing on his ear.

"Silence," snapped his comrade.

The Dreaded One. How totally cool. I had an ass-kicking nickname among the Adamant. I'd done good.

All three continued to step toward me. When they were within a meter, I pointed my laser finger and cut two in half before the third realized my duplicity. He fired point-blank at my face but hit the membrane. I cut him head-to-crotch, and he split almost comically, if it weren't so damn gross.

I jumped for cover and searched for signs of pursuers. None. I listened carefully. Nothing. I was probably home free. I ran in a zig-zag pattern to the trees covering the forested hill. Once there, I again checked for signs of trouble. I smiled. I'd escaped in one piece. I only hoped some of the others in my squad were as fortunate. But, this was war. Nothing good ever happened. The side that lost the least was the side that won. But the winner always lost more than they could bear.

TWENTY

Lesset sipped tea from a solid gold cup and stared rather blankly at the pop-up display table. It depicted the entire front of planets his forces had engaged an hour earlier. This was the forty-third time he stood staring at a display that showed his forces demolishing once functioning and vibrant groups nestled on the once placid surfaces of their home worlds. He'd lost interest in tracking the numbers after his third lopsided victory.

Finally, as if waking from a deep sleep, he spoke harshly. "Report."

Wing Leader Bethalmayus Sandergras stood and walked over to his commander's side. "We are ahead of schedule, Lord. Losses are extremely light, and major resistance is already waning. Two worlds, Sotovir and Nebulanus, offer no further resistance, aside from isolated recalcitrant rebels."

"Fine. And the planet with more robots than living, the one we suspected would be the most trouble?"

"We are winning. Our progress is slowed by their war-droids. Formidable weapons to be certain. It is estimated that if the robots had another two years, they would have produced a sufficient number of war-droids to make our conquest challenging, if not problematic."

Lesset perked his ears. "Who made that treasonous estimate?"

"I believe a computer in the Reiteration Section."

Lesset turned his head to Bethalmayus for the first time. "Someone must have asked the computer to perform that simulation."

Bethalmayus was torn. He knew it was dicey to speak truth to Lesset. He also felt it was an interesting point that some world might have stood a fighting chance against the Adamant if conditions were different.

"Perhaps it was an AI, Lord. Would you like for me to find out for certain?"

He snarled back his lips silently. "No. Let it pass this time. But circulate word. I do not want subversive speculations encouraged at any level by anyone."

"Lord," he returned with a bow.

"And the most populous planet, the humanoid one?"

"Vorpace, Lord. Yes. The conflict proceeds within two percent of our predictions. Most major cities have fallen, and the skies are ours."

"Two percent?" Lesset rested his cup onto its saucer. "That's a large variance for a world with that technical level."

"Yes, it is, but only slightly statistically significant. Whole Master Bingumon attributes the slight delay to the possible presence of The Dreaded One. He is as of ..." He trailed off speaking when he glanced up and noticed Lesset's expression. Shock, hatred, and vehement anger. *Not good*, reflected Bethalmayus. "Is th ... there a ... an *issue*, Lord?"

"Some individual thought it necessary to keep me in the dark when it was possible that the archenemy of the empire was on the ground on Vorpace? Is it no longer an Adamant's duty to use his brain in my service?"

Bethalmayus's outlook went from really bad to extremely awful. "I, to tell the tr ... truttthh just learned of th ... this fact as you c ... called my name alouddd, Lord." He tried to swallow. "I am ... am p ... personally *outraged*, L ... Lord."

"No, Bethalmayus. It is not yours to be outraged. That burden rest solely on my back." He handed his cup and saucer to his assistant. "Hold this while I pour a refill, will you?"

"Of course, Lord." Naturally Bethalmayus held the saucer at arm's length, just in case.

Lesset lifted the large carafe of tea and removed the lid. Steam curled up abundantly from the opening. He reached and hovered the pot over the cup momentarily, then redirected it to above Bethalmayus's head. There he emptied the entire content onto the Wing Leader's scalp. Defying belief, the Wing Leader did not scream in anguish. Lesset returned the carafe to its holder and took his saucer from the trembling Bethalmayus.

"Where was I?" Lesset asked.

"You had just learned of that Jon Ryan might be on Vorpace, Lord."

"Ah yes. Please triple the number of battle cruisers, quadruple the number of long-range wolf scout craft, and quintuple the number of footlings on the ground. I want Jon Ryan. I prefer him alive, but I will settle for him heaped in a basket. Is that clear, Under Footling Bethalmayus? Make certain your replacement here understands that?"

"Lord."

TWENTY-ONE

I slowly climbed the hill, staying low and going slow. Now that I was clear, I wanted to stay that way. I stopped at dusk around three hundred meters altitude. There was a panoramic view from here, and I could see infrared traces of anyone coming. I checked in with Sapale.

"Earthman One to Mamacita," I said into my headset.

Nothing. Hmm. I ran a quick diagnostic on the unit. It was working fine. Maybe they were out of range? Hardly, unless they left the planet. My unit had a range of only a few hundred klicks. I switched to my internal link, like the one I had with the Als.

You there, brood's-mate?

Still nothing. I started to worry. Could they have been overrun? Not likely with the membrane up and the vortex ten feet away.

Sapale, do you copy?

Nada. They were either out of range, which was extremely unlikely, or they had up a full membrane.

Al, you there? Stingray?

No response. Not surprising, since they were with Sapale, duh. But their non-answer supported the notion they were cloaked, since destroying *Stingray* was beyond even the Adamant. But that meant yours truly was completely on his own. Even if I stole a ship, I'd never escape the Adamant's orbital chokehold on the planet. I'd only be able to leave this rock by folding or warping away. Funny, that made me flash on Gorilla Boy. Maybe he was in range? I could call him and *Whoop Ass* back to carry me to safety? Nah. I'd rather be captured and tortured than deal with that addle-brained AI. Some things are worth avoiding. GB was a pass for me.

I really didn't have a list of options, so I hunkered down and made the best of a long wait. Hey, if it was long enough, Ralph could come rescue me. Gallows humor if ever there were. What I really missed then was a can of beans. Yeah, soldiers in combat freezing in the night air ate unheated beans from a can. That's how it was way back when I was human. Funny the things I missed.

I spent the night hacking Adamant communications. I could drop in on quite a bit. What I heard confirmed what I'd experienced myself. The bad guys were kicking butt. Any lingering resistance was quieting, and more forces were on the way. I was impressed to hear The Dreaded One was on Vorpace. The emperor himself instructed every grunt to do their best to capture the unwashed heathen. I was an unwashed heathen. It had to be a promotion of some kind, up from hated scourge. Unfortunately, I learned that dawn would bring selective bombardments of the planet. This was to help suppress resistance, as well as potentially flush me out. Safe areas were delineated, and all ground forces were ordered to be in one before dawn, or they'd be subject to being exploded along with the targets.

I compared the maps of safe areas to my position. None were nearby. I didn't have access to the maps that told me which areas were about to be lit - up, but this far up a hill seemed like an unlikely target. Later that night, I intercepted announcements that similar mop-up bombardments would take place on the other eleven planets included in this operation. Man, these guys were depressingly thorough.

Along with eavesdropping, I tried again to raise Sapale. I also spent the cold night thinking back on happier times. Those would be other times, since the current ones sucked something awful.

First light found me on the move. The fireworks would commence in just under an hour. I wanted to be higher up and tucked into a ravine. I scaled ever-increasing obstacles and kept an ear out for intruders. My progress was fast and unencumbered.

When precisely one percent of the sun had cleared the horizon, all hell broke loose. Fire leapt from the heavens, and the ground cried out in torment as far as my eyes could see. I cursed the Adamant even more, knowing the same insanity was springing to life on eleven other worlds. I cursed myself even more. I'd failed them, too. They could join the club, the swelling ranks of those I'd let down and allowed to die a horrible, pointless death.

When a path of explosions began ascending my hillside, I determined I wasn't going to move. I hoped the blast line went right over me, sparing me from any further testing. I was done.

Then I heard something unexpected. Or rather, I didn't hear what I expected. Slowly at first, then almost as one, the guns in the sky fell silent. I looked up and went to maximal amplification. I had no idea what I was seeing. I'd never seen anything like it in my very long life. There were faint streaks of light, no flames, way high up. They looked like strings of fireflies from a distance. I wondered what they were.

****

In the heavens above Vorpace, as well as its eleven sister-suffering planets, the emptiness of space was replaced with dragons. Big dragons. Some were brilliant silver, others steely gray. One large group was a gleaming bronze, while another clan was a vibrant copper. One, and only one, was the color of purest gold.

They flew gracefully in the airless void, sweeping down on one warship after another. A gossamer trail of fire leapt from their throats and struck the vessels as they passed. Where touched, the hulls vaporized like butter tossed into a raging bonfire. Then the ships exploded with a flash of brilliance before becoming nothing more than the newest additions to the frigid dust occupying endless space.

In a handful of heartbeats, the Adamant fleet was transfigured from unstoppable to unidentifiable. And when the last ship in the sky was gone, the dragons descended like angels of death toward each planet's surface. Adamant forces huddled together and fired off massive, yet ineffectual volleys of power at the oncoming firestorm. Where they stood or lay or hid cowering, the fine-fire touched them, and they were gone. It was as if they had never existed. By ones and twos, by thousands and tens of thousands, they became one with nothingness. Bitter memories of them would linger for decades, but no actual substance of them would ever be detected, seen, smelled, or mourned.

And when the dragons of Nocturnat, along with one lone dragon from Locinar, were finished erasing what had been the scourge of the Adamant from that now blessed segment of the galactic periphery, they soared, calling out in victory. They ascended into the darkness from whence they came, and they disappeared. But, unlike the now dispersed dust of the Adamant war machine, they had not vanished. They had simply returned home after completing their task.

TWENTY-TWO

After the dragons left, I had to confirm that most of the Adamant ground forces were gone. There were no obvious signs, but a frightened wounded animal in hiding was the hardest to deal with. I jogged back into the city and started clearing buildings. At first, I found no one, friend or foe. Then I began collecting the scattered remnants of the police and army units that had been defending the city.

By the time we reached center city, we were about a thousand strong. A few citizens who never evacuated tagged along, too. We ran into no living Adamant. Their corpses were strewn everywhere. The ones I passed had died from typical blast patterns. The one the dragons must have slain were simply gone. When we came upon one of their great war machines, it was only partially present. Massive sections were simply gone, no singe marks or flash scars. Search as we might, we did not locate even one injured Adamant. They were all dead, in the air and on the ground. Most were simply gone.

I had identified the senior officer present and called him over. "Well, Major, it looks like you're in command here. I suggest you choose who will serve just below you and start organizing your forces."

"He returned a salute. What about you, General Ryan. Aren't you in command here?"

"No. For one thing, I'm an alien. You're in the chain of command somewhere. I also won't be hanging around too long, I suspect. When someone senior shows up, you can pass the torch. But until then, you da man.

I grant you a battlefield promotion, but again, I'm not *your* senior officer."

"Fine, sir. Will do. If you'll excuse me, I have a society to rebuild."

"That's the spirit," I said, returning his salute.

Sapale, are you there? Do you copy?

Still nothing. I decided I'd better make the trek to HQ to see if anything was left intact. Even as I departed, the major was forming up platoons and sending them off in various directions to explore. The civilians were tasked with scrounging for food and water. Exactly what I'd have done.

The city wasn't in complete ruin, but it was pretty torn up. A few habitable structures remained, but most would have to be razed to make room for the new eventually. When I came across stragglers, I directed them toward city center. If what I observed was typical, then a lot of the humans had survived. Intermittently, I called out to Sapale, but I never heard a peep back. Another town square was functioning as the aggregation point for military and civilian survivors. I found the woman who appeared to be in charge.

"Yo, there's another gather spot in the square about a klick that way."

"St. Germain's Garden, the one with the old clock tower?" she asked.

"Yeah, that's the one. Only a third of an old tower now."

"Damn Adamant. No respect for useless old monuments." She turned to a soldier close by. "Hanzell, get over to Saint Germain's and let them know we're here. Leave them your radio if they don't have one."

"Ma'am." He saluted and jogged away.

"So you're the android, right?"

I leaned over and extended my hand. "Jon Ryan. Nice to meet you."

"Anchee Payette," she responded shaking back. She smirked. "Never met a legend before."

"Want me to sign some concealed body part?"

"Nah, I'm good. Hey, you see any live Adamant since that whatever it was?"

"Nope. Only the ones we killed before the dragons magically puffed them away."

"Come again."

"Those were flying fire-breathing dragons that vaporized the entire invasion force. It was a miracle. Didn't you see them?"

She stared at me in disbelief a moment. "Yeah, little tiny ones with flowers glued to their butts." She spaced her fingers a couple inches apart and held them up. "Ryan, did you take any shrapnel to the head?"

Once I got a look at HQ, or rather what was left of it, I knew why those present jumped into *Stingray* and split. The building was a wreck. The large situation room was even worse. There were signs of an intense firefight, but there were also clear indications the place had been ransacked roughly after the fighting stopped. Of course, ripping apart your enemy's command center was a good idea. I was impressed yet again with Adamant thoroughness.

I figured the vortex was gone, not just under a full membrane, but I decided to check. I meticulously went around the room, poking my rifle into every space to see if bounced off some invisible object. In the end, there was nothing. Sapale had taken the vortex somewhere. Oh well. She'd hear of the bizarre victory sooner or later and return, probably to HQ itself. I could kick back and wait for their return. Plus, I had time to make up a wild story about how I single-handedly saved the day. If given enough time, I'd concoct a cock-and-bull story excluding the dragons altogether. All right, I was in my wheelhouse.

A few hours later, *Stingray* silently appeared. Crap. I hadn't had time to tighten up the weaker aspects of my BS tale. The hull formed a portal, and Sapale cautiously stuck her head around to sneak a peek. Instead of bloodthirsty Adamant, she saw me, feet up on a table, wiggling my fingers in greeting.

"There you are," I said nonchalantly, "you were almost late for dinner. I'd give the soufflé five minutes *tops* before it's into the garbage."

She relaxed and stepped out of *Stingray*. "Soufflé? Do you know what I'd really like? An explanation as to what the fuck happened. One minute we're fighting for our lives, and the next you're sitting here with that cat-eating-shit grin on your face I've hated for billions of years."

I shrugged and turned my palms up silently replying, *what can I say.*

Shielan was next out. She swept the room with her rifle until she was sure it was safe. "Y'all can come out now. The room's secure."

"Shie-shie" asked Sapale, "may I borrow your weapon?"

She flicked her head and tossed it over. Sapale rested it not so gently on my forehead. "You have three seconds. What happened, or I shoot. And if you give me your BS version of how you single-handedly ..."

I eased the gun off my skin. "Okay," I cut her off, "it was the Plezrite. They appeared out of nowhere and destroyed the entire bleeping Adamant force."

"Could you release my gun, so I can shoot you."

"No, Sapale, it's Davdiad's own truth. Once we're outside, you can randomly stop someone in the street and ask them."

Her stern face softened. "Are you okay?"

I pointed to my chest. "Me? Are you serious? Of course, I'm okay. I'm Jon *Freaking* Ryan."

She whacked me alongside the head with the rifle and then threw it back to Shielan. "How soon after we left did they show up?"

"I don't know when you split. The Plezrite struck at dawn, here and on the other eleven planets under attack."

She whistled softly. "That's a lot of dragons."

"Millions."

Sapale was silent, but I knew *exactly* what she was thinking. With a Plezrite army of millions, we could wipe the Adamant out as a species. We could reclaim our galaxy and restore order and justice.

Then she shook her head to clear it. "What did they say? Why did they wait until the second day after millions were slaughtered?"

"They never said a word. When the Adamant were no more, they left."

"Don't make me retrieve that weapon," she menaced.

"Serious as a bullet to the face, they never made contact. They just did their thing and disappeared."

"Why would they do that?" asked Jonnaha as she stepped out of *Stingray*.

"Maybe because they did it for their own reasons, not to save us. They figured they didn't need our permission, thanks, or praise to help themselves."

"Makes sense, I guess," she replied. "It does suggest they aren't interested in joining in our alliance. That's a crying shame. Next time, we might not be so lucky."

Damn, Jonnaha was right. I hadn't thought of it yet, but did I really believe we'd defeated the Adamant? If I knew them, and I did, they'd be back in greater number and with worse attitudes. Then if the Plezrite didn't show, the twelve planets would be toast. Total armageddon, no one left alive and no blade of grass unsinged.

"We need to find out for sure, don't we?" I said standing.

"We absolutely must," responded Jonnaha.

"What, are we going to Nocturnat now?" asked Sapale.

"Why wouldn't we?" asked Jonnaha.

"Because your world is in ruins, and you're the leader, maybe."

"If the Plezrite aren't fully onboard, the rubble out there and those who stand upon it are doomed anyway."

"She's right," I said. "All aboard who's coming along."

We all piled into the cube and headed for the Plezrite home world. They were going to be pissed when we got there, bringing more aliens to know where they lived. They might fry us all and be done with the lot of us intruders for good.

I set down where I had when I brought Cala. Knowing she had that spooky brindas insight, I figured if she wasn't there anyway she would be when she sensed our presence. Man, did I look smart or what? I stepped out of *Stingray* and nearly collided with the gorgeous golden girl herself, sitting in her statue pose.

"Cala, you old witch, I'd give you a big hug, but I might stab myself to death," I said by way of greeting.

"How reassuring. One less thing to worry about in this sad life," she replied.

"My lord, she's *beautiful*," marveled Jonnaha when she came out.

Shielan stepped out right behind her sister. "Nice lizard there, Ryan."

"Curse the Fates and Realms," said Cala, "there are *two* of them in the universe."

"I don't know what you're talking about, but I'll take that as a compliment, ma'am."

"*Ma'am*? Don't make me regret convincing the Plezrite to save your sorry world, child."

Shielan gave me a what-the-hell shrug and went over to her sister's side.

"Cala, if I may address you as such, thank you for—"

Cala raised a hand. "Thanks are not necessary. We will talk at length, I am certain. But let us do so in a more comfortable setting. Come." With that, Cala turned and walked toward a nearby building. We followed closely behind.

Yisbid sat at a round table. Cala sat next to her and signaled that we should sit where we wanted. There were just us six in the room.

"May I get you anything?" asked Yisbid.

We all shook our heads.

"No, we're fine," said Jonnaha. I guess she felt, as the chief political muckety-muck, it was her place to speak for us. That was fine by me. I'd spearheaded more than my share of "important" meetings, thank you very much. "I want to start by—"

"*I* will start, child," Yisbid interrupted in a formal tone. "We have much to discuss, but I feel it's best to state our position first. We struck at the Adamant for purely selfish reasons. I was shown a future by my friend Cala, in which we were subjugated by the evil beasts. We acted to prevent that future."

I couldn't stand it. Sorry, I mean I had to say it. "Cala, you have a *friend*? Will wonders never cease?"

Cala turned to face Yisbid. "You remember the lessons I taught you about restraint and internal strength? This one is an excellent test for those abilities."

"Perhaps we should invite him to stay so many might master that skill?"

Cala shook her big head. "The gain would never be worth the price. Trust me on this."

"Aw, you two are verging on insulting me."

Cala stared at me. "If only that were possible. However, I think we should return to the important discussion we are here to have."

"Your planet, your call," I replied, looking away. Shielan, bless her heart, snickered. Sapale elbowed me hard.

"As I was saying," continued Yisbid, "we acted to avert the unthinkable. But, as each action spawns a series of reactions, I must say we did so once. We are not prepared to do it again."

I needed to speak. We, *I*, needed these guys. "Wait a hold-on second. You assumed it was those isolated Adamant you killed who posed a threat to you? I only ask rhetorically because you know you cannot make that assumption. If you want to stop them from ending *you*, you need to end *them*. It's just that simple, and I bet you know it."

Yisbid got such a sad look in her eyes. I believe forlorn would be the word that covered it. "You are wise, Jon Ryan. I must grant you that."

"We know that removing a large but probably inconsequential segment of their war machine did not end their threat to us," said Cala.

"Or anyone else," I added.

"Jon, you know firsthand what happened to the Deft of Locinar. They were permanently removed as a threat. Similarly, you know that the Plezrite went to great lengths to hide their position. Even *I* did not know of their existence. Do you know why these two events took place? How they converge?"

"Not a single clue," I responded honestly.

"Because we are such a great threat to anyone with malice in their hearts. If the Adamant would dominate all they can touch, we would have to be eliminated. The Deft were, and the Plezrite hid themselves assiduously. If they had not, they would have been destroyed."

"So, you must see that if we persist in fighting the Adamant, they will eventually come to know our location, and they will direct whatever force it takes to exterminate us as they did the Deft," said an impassioned Yisbid. "For us, to fight is to die."

"But you did fight," responded Jonnaha.

"Yes. Once. We did so with great reservation, but we felt it was worth the risk," replied Cala. "We hurt them badly. We pray the confusion and apprehension that their stunning defeat produces will make them cautious about making war in this region again."

"And for now, at least, they know only where the Plezrite struck, not where they live." Yisbid raised her arms demonstrably. "We are a very long way from there, and few know where we are."

I didn't totally like the way she said *few*. Let me see. Sapale, me, and the Als knew where we were. Jonnaha and Shielan knew that they were somewhere, though they had no real notion as to where they were. But they knew there was a planet somewhere with lots of dragons. If the Adamant captured them, that would be enough to start the search for the Plezrite. Okay, that was the complete list of *few*, and they were all sitting across from fire-breathing dragons. Well, the Als weren't, but they couldn't move if both Sapale and I were, um, *neutralized*. What was it they were always saying in the *Star Wars* series? *I've got a bad feeling about this*, I believe were the exact words. I penciled myself in for that line, too.

The same thing must have hit Sapale. "Calfada-Joric, I call on you formally. You owe me a blood debt. My brood-mate saved the last two Deft, so you owe me two blood debts. As they live on and their family—*your* family—grows as we speak, the final number you owe is yet to be written. I will hold you to those debts until you've paid them off."

Cala lowered her head and spoke. "I am but one. One soul, one vote, one dissenting voice. I bear the weight of your charges, but I am not in a position to do anything to alter the present."

"Then come sit by my side," I said with all the bravado I ever had rolled into one bold overreaching invitation. On cue, Sapale rose to leave an empty seat next to me and sat next to Shielan.

Cala looked up at me and damn she'd have smiled if she'd had the right muscles to do so. There was a glint of joy in her eyes. She stood and flapped her massive wings. Instead of walking around the table, the big show-off walked on the table. She flicked one wing and landed gently in the seat by me.

"You know what?" I said to her as I patted her arm. "I think I love you."

"Ah, sound motivation for my death has now presented itself. Thank the Maker of Right."

"Cala," said Yisbid in a hushed tone. "It does not have to be like this. it does not have to end as such. You are of great value to us. You are, in fact, priceless. Do not forfeit what you represent in an act of haste."

"I am not priceless, child," she responded. "This man," she thumped me on the shoulder, "*he* is priceless. As is this brave woman of Kaljax." She nodded to Sapale. "And these proud sisters are worth ten of me in the eyes of the divine," she said looking to Jonnaha and Shielan. "It would be an honor and high privilege to die at their sides, in their service."

There was an electronic whine as Shielan powered up her blaster. God love her, she was the very picture of consistency.

Yisbid rose. Behind us, a column of Plezrite visants filed into the room. That mega-bitch Himanai led the line. Knowing I still held Risrav, their magic was unlikely to work on me. They'd have to club me to death. Good. That'd give me more than enough time to put lots of holes in that waste of space's hide.

"We do not act lightly or with a clear conscience," said Yisbid. "We do what we must to defend our legacy, the lengthy line of Plezrite who—"

"The self-righteous betrayer will be silent," boomed through the room. The walls shook. Everyone spun to see who spoke. In the doorway stood a pure white dragon, gleaming like pure ice struck by a brilliant beam of light.

"What is the meaning …" Yisbid never finished her sentence. Well, I guess she might have, wherever it was she disappeared to, assuming for her sake she wasn't just deleted.

"Is there another who would open their treacherous mouth and spew vile abominations?" asked the white dragon.

"I will know who you are," demanded Himanai.

"Yes, I suppose you will, though it will not benefit you in any way. I am the brindas Mirraya-Slapgren. More importantly, I am extremely pissed. Those who have stirred my wrath should be very afraid."

Cala made as if to speak but relaxed back before doing so. I believe she was ceding the floor to her best pupil.

"Your evil tricks and twisted …" That was all for Himanai. *Poof,* and good riddance.

"How many are you in number, you corruptors of all that is good and decent in our species?" Mirri asked of the nearest dragon.

"You can make a handful of us disappear, but you cannot defeat a planet of Plezrite. I now speak for all our people. You are unwelcome scum, and you will all die miserably," replied the unwise visant. Boy, I wouldn't want to be her right about then.

"You do, do you?" challenged Mirri. "Let us see if that is true." She closed her eyes and strained visibly.

Cala leaned over to me and whispered. "She is linking the minds of the Plezrite with hers. I too hear her words. She asks if all the Plezrite agree with Hoiney. She's the visant who just spoke."

"What are the locals saying back?" I asked, with considerable personal interest in the answer.

"They are collectively *shocked*," Cala spoke in wonder. "Here. I'll let Mirri tell you."

"I have learned that only you few criminals have dared to betray your citizens. No one else knew of your treachery. You seven have been denied."

Several of the remaining rebel Plezrite gasped.

"It's a big deal," whispered Cala. Man, she had a smug look of satisfaction on her face.

"I will carry out your denial. You will be sent to Locinar, where I banished the other two criminals. There, you will see if your plots and evil souls serve you well, or not at all."

And they were gone.

"Excellent work, my friend," said Cala to Mirri. "Even I'm impressed."

"Hey, I need to know," I said to Mirri, "is it safe to hug you?"

"I don't know, Uncle Jon. Let's find out." She opened her arms and her wings, and I dived in with abandon. I did run a system's check while doing so. No leaks.

"Slapgren, you in there, too?" I asked her chest.

"Of course, you bozo," Mirri replied. "We are one."

"You're welcome," I said, and I hugged them some more. Sapale and the others piled on, too. It was … nice.

TWENTY-THREE

Lesset stared blankly at the giant holoscreen at the center of the Lead Point Room. He was daydreaming of the acquisition, control, and expansion of his power. He was not paying strict attention to the battle that was raging into its second day. By all accounts, the campaign was wildly successful and all but over. Soon he'd present himself to that dwarf-brained emperor and receive more useless medals and further land grants. He'd take more wives and sire more worthless pups. But then he'd begin the next plan for—

Something caught his attention indirectly. At first Lesset couldn't put a name to it, the distraction. He shook his head and flipped on his intense, unerring focus. What? What was different? There, one of the lights on the screen flashed. It was a large dot. Dots on the holoscreen never blinked, flashed, or did anything but burn brightly.

"Guvrof," he snapped, pointing at his adjutant.

Guvrof vaulted to his feet and sped to Lesset's side. "Sir?"

"That light there, why's it blinking?"

"I don't rightly know, sir. I've never seen that before. It's probably a malfunction, maybe a bad emitter."

"No, look there." he pointed emphatically. "Another one's started flashing.

Guvrof stepped to the holoscreen. He slapped a technician seated at a large control panel at the screen's base. "You there, what does the flashing light mean?"

"What flashing light, sir?" He looked up and rubbed his eyes.

"You *idiot*, that one there and there. Those two blinking lights."

"Flashing lights indicate a damaged vessel. If the ship's okay, the light stays at the same intensity. If the light switches from flashing to a simple ring, it means … there, you see the ring of light?"

"Yes, of course I do. What does it mean?"

"The ship's been destroyed."

Guvrof was momentarily stunned into silence. "Ah, that's not possible. Which ship is that?"

"*Was* that, Wedge Leader." He tapped a few buttons. "That *was* the *Never Know Defeat*."

"She's a dreadnaught. She can't be destroyed. She's eighteen million tons of firepower and shielding."

"That's what … there, see the other light is now a ring."

"Which ship …"

The technician was already tapping keys frantically. "*House of Pain*, sir."

"She's a battle-class destroyer. Also impossible."

"Guvrof," shouted Lesset, "report immediately."

He walked slowly to his commander, puzzling what to say. If he passed along false information, it'd be his head. If he withheld information, it'd be his head. If he passed along bad news, it'd be his head.

"Sir, the technician sitting there," he pointed out the specific individual should blame need quick assignment, "claims a flashing light indicates a damaged ship."

"And the thin circle of light?" Lesset thundered.

"*He* maintains the ring indicates a destroyed vessel. Granted, the fellow must be wrong. I think—"

"Which ships?" Lesset cut off his ranting.

"*Never Know Defeat* and *House of Pain*, sir."

Lesset had never heard of *two* ships lost. It was inconceivable. To lose one was a rarity, but two called sanity into question.

"Get me the Watch Commander here *now*," barked Lesset.

Guvrof scurried away quickly. Lesset looked to the screen again. It was becoming filled with flashing lights. Soon, there were no solid lights and dozens upon dozens of flashing lights switched to circles every time he blinked. He could not be seeing what he was seeing.

Guvrof literally pushed the Watch Commander in front of him as they approached Lesset.

"What is the meaning of this outrage, Sub-Wedge Spliter? Who is entering this false information?" demanded Lesset.

"No one, Lord. The data stream is fully automated and cannot be tampered with. The status arrives directly from each ship's encrypted transponder. It cannot be altered in any way."

"Do you mean to tell me that most of our ships above twelve separate planets are being simultaneously wiped out? Is that what you are saying?" The veins in Lesset's neck bulged ominously as he screamed.

"I … I am saying *nothing*, Lord. I am telling you the system is automated and is reporting what it was designed to do." The dog was trembling like he was freezing to death.

"Then your system is malfunctioning." He raised an accusatory finger under the commander's nose. "I am holding you personally responsible. Do you hear me?"

"Lord, please understand …"

"I do not need to understand anything other than your *complete* incompetence."

A junior officer ran up. "High Wedge, I have received audio reports from multiple ships." He held out a data chit.

Lesset looked at the device very carefully before he took it from the officer. He grabbed his handheld and attached the drive.

This is Wedge Leader Ventelot of the cruiser Magnificent Victory *reporting. We are under attack by *** ships that are *** the design of larger dragons. They *** directed some new beam *** us that *** unable to stop. We've *** all forward shielding and *** hull breaches …*

Only static followed.

Wedge Leader Lesset, Himalfi here from what's left of the Resist All. *We're ...*
Only static followed.

Dragons, Lord, are attacking our flotilla. I've lost ...
Only static followed.

"This is preposterous," Lesset howled as he handed his handheld to Guvrof. "Contact each of those morons and find out what is the matter with their *brains.*"

"At once, Lord." Guvrof gladly sped away.

"Get me Field Whole Descanfor immediately," Lesset yelled to the nearest officer.

Within seconds, a panicky voice came from the speakers. "Lesset, is that *you?* Gods and demons, it's all going wrong. I see our ships raining down from the sky like leaves from autumn trees in a storm. Lesset, you have to send me reinforcements at once. My troops are disappearing. Do you hear me ...?"

"Shut up and listen, you half breed. Report to me what is going on. You're raving like a mad fool."

"There's no time. Lesset, we're all ..."

Only a static hiss could be heard.

"Will somebody *tell* me what in the Fires of Death is going on?" Lesset's grip on reality was slipping away.

Guvrof ran back. "Lord, I cannot raise a single vessel. They ... they all appear to be lost. I heard scattered mention of dragons attacking, but then all transmissions ..."

BANG.

The sound was followed with Guvrof's head exploding in a cloud of red mist. Lesset holstered his sidearm.

"I will hear no *nonsense* about dragons flying in outer space. Someone bring me a correct report."

Every head in the Lead Point Room was craned down as far as it could go. All eyes were on either the floor or the desktop. Silence reigned, aside from the background electronic hum.

Lesset pulled his pistol out again. He pointed it in a jerking manner around the room. "Will no one come to the aid of his leader? Are you all traitorous dogs?"

Their eyes remained down.

Lesset placed the barrel in his mouth and pulled the trigger.

A senior officer bolted into the room. "Emperor Palawent has called and demanded a report on the batt ..." He trailed off as he saw the headless remains of what were the two highest-ranking officers heaped together on the floor.

TWENTY-FOUR

"Jon, I can't *believe* you called me directly. Do you know how insanely dangerous that is for me?" hissed Harhoff.

"Oh, trust me, brother, you're going to thank me in a few seconds. I had to tell you this personally. And if you die right after, you'll die a happy puppy," I responded.

"No, I won't. Whenever I die, it will be begrudgingly and with purely negative emotions. Go ahead, what's so damn important?"

"What size do you wear. I'm Christmas shopping, and think I found the perfect gift for you."

"Not funny. What?"

"You know the attack on the periphery, the one you alerted me was being moved ahead of schedule?"

"Me, too," whined Garustfulous from behind. "I helped in *every* phase of that mission."

"Will you shut up and let the man speak. Man," commanded Harhoff, "*speak.*"

"Well, the operation went less stunningly than it was drawn out on paper."

"Meaning?" snapped Harhoff impatiently.

"The entire expeditionary force was wiped out. Every ship, every foot soldier, and every shit-shoveler. They're all gone."

"Jon, you know I am among the few who appreciate your sense of humor. But this is not—"

"I figured you might not believe me, so I'm sending you this." I wagged a data chit in the air, then I inserted it in a slot and flicked a switch.

"What is this?" he asked as he tapped controls.

"It's a holo of the sky above one of the twelve planets attacked. Gabdorna, to be specific. It was taken a few hours ago, just after dawn."

"Jon, I don't know what I'm supposed to be seeing. These are just meteors or something."

"Those aren't meteors. Well, hang on, I guess technically they are by that point. What they began life as was the entire flotilla sent to attack and subdue Gabdorna. They are falling from the sky because after they exploded, their engines weren't stopping gravity from doing its thing."

Garustfulous shouted over Harhoff. "Are you saying the entire force was destroyed? That's not possible."

"It's possible because it happened. I assume the powers that be will try and keep this under wraps as long as possible. I wanted you to know the truth right away. Dude, this is *so* big."

"Thank you for thinking of me in that regard, Jon," replied Garustfulous.

"I was speaking to Harhoff. You know that, right?"

"Er, of course. You're not the only one trying to make funny," he responded, deflated.

"How could such a one-sided victory have occurred?" asked Harhoff.

"Magic dragons, that's how."

"Ah, well why didn't you say so to begin with? Of course, it was magical dragons." I think my friend was skeptical.

"I figured you'd have trouble swallowing that, too, so I brought along one to show you." I stepped aside and pulled Mirri into the picture. "Harhoff, meet Mirraya-Slapgren. Mirraya-Slapgren, meet Harhoff. He doesn't believe in magical dragons."

"No," she said, "is that true, Harhoff? I could see not buying the whole Santa Claus and Tooth Fairy thing, but enchanted dragons? Everyone believes in us."

"Jon, is that thing a holo-projection. So help me—"

Harhoff stopped yelling when a bucket of liquid dumped itself on his head.

He spewed spit and slapped at his muzzle.

"Would you like to see additional magic, friend Harhoff? asked Mirri cheerily.

"No, I'm now a believer. Thanks. I'm sure I needed a bath anyway."

"Gee," Mirri replied placing a talon on her lower lip, "I didn't send water, did I?"

"Don't bother telling me. I believe in you, and I believe that was the purest water. Jon, get back on screen."

"You called?"

"So that dragon was able to defeat an entire attack force? Please excuse me if I'm incredulous."

"Harhoff, I'll give it to you straight. I can't tell you more. You will learn whatever your leaders choose to tell you. I wanted you to know why the defeat was so complete."

He tossed his head side to side. "Understandable. Need to know and all that."

"Precisely."

"I suppose you're proud of yourself?"

I held up pinched fingers. "Just this much."

"And I suppose you think this will be the death-knell of the Adamant Empire?"

"That would be nice."

He rubbed his chin. "Well, if anything might do it, this would be it. We shall have to see."

"Indeed, we shall," I replied. "But, Harhoff."

"Yes?"

"I gotta say it's so totally cool. I'm like *completely* jazzed."

"I'll assume those are positive things."

I held up the pinched fingers again. "Just this much."

TWENTY-FIVE

Mirraya, Slapgren had separated back to themselves. Cala and those two had a decision to make. It was a big one. Were they going to return to Rameeka Blue Green or remain on Nocturnat? Were they going to hold with the past or commit to a new life among their own kind? If asked, duh, I'd have given my opinion. But they worked it out themselves, the three of them. After weighing pros and cons, they decided to move permanently to Nocturnat. There were thousands of visants anxious to learn the ways of the brindas. It turned out that there was a societal party-line about rejecting the Deft ways, but it was just that. Denying the study of magic was a phrase repeated for generations, but there was no emotion *invested* in it. Presently, no one alive had the slightest idea what it was they were supposed to stand against. The prejudices of a million years ago, when the schism occurred, were as dead as the people who felt them passionately. Go figure.

The five of us sat down over coffee when they announced their decision.

"We're going to move the children here and assimilate ourselves into the Plezrite society," Mirri said with a bright smile. "I miss my people, as does Slapgren. Our family will benefit from a more normal experience."

"For the record, as witnessed by the recent near-calamity, I do not miss my people and would rather live apart." I don't know if I believed Cala, but I would expect her to say just that, grizzly old bat that she was. "But I need to see to the completion of these two's education." She tossed her head in their direction.

"That may or may not be necessary," responded Mirri. "But there are many to teach, and we are but two. Your service to your race is needed now more than ever."

"Plus, Mirri's got a bunch of kids to tend to," added Slapgren. "For the time being, she's only a part-time teacher."

"I must have been a *wicked* person in a former life," sighed Cala, "to suffer endless punishment ... and me being such a wonderful individual."

"Speaking of endless punishment, Uncle Jon ..." Mirri let the sentence fade.

"Yeah, I almost forgot." I took a big swig of coffee and thudded the mug down. "I got a little more than two months before my debt comes due."

"You could turn yourself in now, cut out the tense anticipation," said Cala.

Slapgren snickered. "You two will be at each other until the end of time. I'm convinced of it."

"*He* may be present at the end of time, but I'll be resting comfortably in my grave long before that, thank you very much," replied Cala as she gestured toward me.

"If I didn't know better, I'd start getting a little jealous right about now," Sapale said as she looked back and forth between Cala and me.

"Me and that revolting looking human a pair? *Bah*. I have some standards, I'll have you know."

"Okay then. I can rest easily tonight," Sapale replied with a crooked smile.

"Seriously, Uncle Jon, what's your next move? I can't see you marching through the gates of hell without a fight, a plan, or a con," Slapgren said.

"What is it with the 'what's your plan,'" I protested. "Who says a plan to avoid the inevitable is even possible?"

"Yeah," he responded. "So, what's your plan?"

"He won't even tell me," Sapale said coolly. "He says if the shocking details got out, the entire house of burning cards might come tumbling down." She rolled her eyes. Man, she was cute.

"Well, if there's any way we can help, Uncle Jon, you have to promise to ask," said Mirri.

"I will," I said, grabbing my mug between both palms. Without intending to, I crushed it to pieces. The little coffee that was in it splattered to the table.

"Why is it I don't believe you?" asked Mirraya.

"Hey, someone slips me a defective mug and all of the sudden I'm not asking for help from those I love?"

"You're free to ask me, too, you know." That Cala, she never missed a chance to zap me.

"Here's an idea," said Mirri. "Why don't all of you leave Uncle Jon and me alone? He may speak more freely if there's no crowd."

"What?" sputtered Sapale. "I'm his mate of two *billion* years. If he is going to open up to anyone, it's damn sure going to be *me*."

"I, however, might be in a superior place to aid him. Perhaps he requires more than a welcome ear."

Sapale studied my face. She was hot, and she was hurt. But then I saw it dawn on her. She loved me enough to want what was best for me. She slid her hand on top of mine. "I'll be in *Blessing* when you're ready," she said. She got up and left in silence.

Cala and Slapgren did the same. It was just me and my little girl, Mirri. I couldn't put the image of the first time I saw her all those years ago on the prison ship out of my mind. Her clutching her dead brother with a look of total despair. My how the worm had turned.

"How may I help, dearest uncle?"

"I need to find EJ."

"I did not anticipate that. May I ask why?"

"Yes, but I won't tell you, so don't ask."

She nodded and smiled faintly. "Very well. It's your call. How do you plan on finding him?"

"I have no idea." I looked down at the table. "It's a big galaxy out there."

"Do you suspect he's looking for you?"

"I thought of that. Sure, he wants to find me to take Risrav and dismember me. But I can't bank on him finding me in time. Even if I broadcast my location with a bullhorn and shined floodlights on myself, he might take too long."

"I agree. I suppose you could ask the rune."

"Huh?"

"I said you could ask Risrav where Varsir is."

I shook my head. "Is that even remotely possible?"

She shrugged. "I'm not certain. In theory, perhaps."

"If it did, why hasn't EJ used that ability to find me?"

She got a very smug look on her face. "Who says he hasn't? Hmm? He did sneak up on you on Kaljax and shot you in the back, I believe you told me."

"Yeah, but he was there for Sapale. He was with her."

"And she was with you."

"No, I came separately."

"If you say so."

"What do you mean *if I say so*? It's a fact. I arrived after she and he were already there. I brought the kids to her."

"I might claim you were linked. I might even say you two have been linked since the day you met."

"What does that mean? Seriously?"

"If you are linked, your fates are intertwined."

"I'm beginning to see why the Plezrite dumped you brindases. You talk good double-speak but say so little."

"We could argue this point until your Ralph comes to claim you. Why don't you just try? It can't hurt if I'm proven correct ... except for your pride."

Touché. She was right. "Could you please turn your head?"

"I beg your pardon?"

"I said turn your head, girl. I'm going to retrieve the rock, and I don't want an audience."

"You have never and will never change."

"Not if I can help it."

I winked. She turned. I retrieved.

"Here, you try," I said handing her the stone.

She threw her arms up. "No. It's in *your* custody, not mine. You ask it."

"Can I buy a clue as to how?"

"First, you must boil equal parts goat's blood and oil of primrose. Then add one tail of newt."

"Seriously?"

"No. I suggest you simply ask your rune." She pointed to it.

"Sure. What the hell, right?"

"That's the spirit. How is failure possible?"

"Smart ass kid. You're not too big to spank you know?

"Someone's stalling."

I grumbled loudly because she was correct again. How very annoying.

"Hey, rock, where's your counterpart?" I asked it as it sat in my palm. After a few seconds I turned to Mirri. "Not very chatty today, I guess."

"Try and be serious for ten consecutive seconds."

I grumbled louder. I really should spank the brat. I looked at the rune. I focused on its rough surface, the scattered pits and chips of mica. I turned it so the light reflected off it in different ways. Funny, I'd never noticed how pretty the rock was. It held secrets I hadn't considered. It was old. The rune was very old, older than me. It held great pain. How a stone could hold pain was beyond me, but I *saw* it as plainly as I saw my own hand.

The rune longed to be with its other half, its split, its finisher. It pined to be with Varsir. But it could not be. Varsir was so far away. It was so very removed that the pain inside both runes could not be assuaged. Only if they could be together would their suffering end. If only Risrav could be ..."

"They're on Kantawir. EJ and Varsir are on the planet Kantawir. It's in the Hantorian System."

"Very impressive, Uncle. You asked, and the rune answered. I'm very proud of you."

"But there just one problem."

"What?"

"He now knows I'm coming for him."

"Do you think he'll take flight?"

"No, I know he won't. He's waiting for me."

"That could present a problem."

I slipped the rune in my pocket. "Ya think?"

TWENTY-SIX

The twelve new members of the Secure Council were huddled around the table, hunched over and silent. They were all acutely aware that their promotions were a result of the lightning quick vacancies resulting from what was being called unofficially The Disgrace of Our Race. All were anxious to avoid the gruesome, gory ends that their predecessors had suffered because of the disastrous, unprecedented loss. Not a single new officer on the council campaigned for their seat. They were, in fact, the senior officers who least effectively avoided selection.

To add to the discredit and impossible assignment the Secure Council now faced, the emperor himself presided over the first meeting. No emperor was *ever* invited to, desired at, or allowed to attend these meetings. The sessions were too important for political hacks to muck up the necessary work. So, humiliation was added to the anxiety and misgiving already apparent in the newly elected military leaders.

"We are not pleased to have to interrupt our busy schedule to be here today," began a clearly intoxicated Emperor Palawent. "But since the former occupants of these previously honorable seats were so inconsequent ... *incompetent*, so treacherous, and so intensely stupid as to lose a battle that any *puppy* could have won if blindfolded and had to make decisions while being beaten with a switch." He stopped talking, apparently feeling he'd completed some thought. His body language challenged anyone to say word, which of course, no one wanted to in the first place.

"That's better," he said, spitting saliva over those most closely positioned to him. Again, he seemed to be under the mistaken impression he'd made some important, complete point. "Now I want each and every one of you *princesses* in pink skirts to swear your allegiance to me here and now," he pointed to the withered Loserandi standing beside him, "in the face of god or whatever." The motion of turning rapidly in one direction and then the reverse almost caused him to fall from his chair. Fortunately, the armrests were oversized.

Calran Klug, the new Prime of the council, raised a paw, albeit sheepishly.

"What Krulug Run? Do you have a question, or do you need to go pee?" The emperor kicked his legs in the air, he was so smitten with his humor.

"My Imperial Lord, we would all be honored to pledge our undying allegiance to you *again*. But, if you will recall we did so for the second time today not ten minutes ago. Would you like the holo replayed?"

"No, I ... We do not want the *holo* replayed. We want the loyalty of your incompetent, inconsequential, inept, in ... in ... what other *in* word am I ... we're forgetting?" He tried to snap his fingers but was too drunk to generate a sound.

Not surprisingly, no syntactical assistance was offered.

"Fine," slurred Palawent. "If there are no further take, we shall questions our leave?" He pointed as best he could aim at each member individually. "You had better impress the crap out of me. If you don't, I'll make what I did to those p ... p ... pork chops you replaced look like a picnic in the park where they serve pork chops." He squealed in rapture at his wit. Palawent, not surprisingly, squealed alone.

"Yes, My Imperial Lord. We thank you for your wisdom and your irreplaceable time. We have all benefitted from your very presence today," responded Calran Klug most unconvincingly.

Two of his aides helped walk/drag the emperor from the council chamber. Exiting the door, he belched loudly and said, "I think that went ..." Then he passed out for the third time that morning.

"Demons and blood ticks," spat Calran Klug once the doors were shut, "we are in an *impossible*, completely untenable position here. How are we supposed to get this war machine out of the *sewer* with insufferable interference like that?"

"Mind your words, old friend," said Darfos, a Whole Leader who'd known the new Prime for decades. "Closed doors are not enough to guarantee privacy, times as they are." He made a show of glancing around the table.

"Do you mean to suggest one of us might stab another in the back, Darfos?"

"Or in the front if it allows him to survive this gantlet we're stuck in," he replied.

"If we don't watch each other's backs, we're all going to die soon and uncomfortably." He scanned the room. "You all know this, right?"

No one bothered to pretend to disagree.

"Well, if you didn't then, know it now. If any of us are to live, we must be united in every sense of the word." Wisely, he did not follow his initial impulse and ask for a vote on the matter then and there. Damn it, he thought, why couldn't *he* have been assigned to one of the ships that was destroyed?

"In any case," said Darfos, "I believe it would be best if we proceeded with our usual business."

"Nothing will ever be *usual* again. Our business is to *live*. If we piece together a fleet, and if that fleet wins victories, that's all fine and well. But my vision of success is to do as little as possible, so we can be held accountable for as little as possible."

"Surely you realize those words are *treasonous*," spoke Nalvir, a dimwitted Wedge Commander of paw soldiers.

"Not if no one outside these walls *hears* them," replied Calran Klug.

"If you are suggesting we conspire ..."

"Shut up, Nalvir," snapped Darfos. "Bravado and lofty words won't keep you alive a second longer than the rest of us. It will come as no surprise to anyone present that no one present wanted to serve on the Secure Council. We were the idiots who did not take one step backward when the call came for volunteers to step forward. Get over yourself and focus on life, yours *and* your family's."

Those words did make even the boorish Nalvir take full notice.

"All right," continued the Prime, "I could call for nominations and hold secret elections, but why the hell bother? Darfos, you're the Vice Prime. Lopeth, you're First Recorder. Japjad, you will serve as Counter. All in favor signify by not saying a thing or making any single sound whatsoever."

Silence followed.

"The motion is carried unanimously. Our next task is to inventory the remaining craft and personnel still under our command."

"But wait," interrupted Sevrop, a young naval officer with a family not influential enough to spare him this job. "You know as well as the rest of us the armada sent out represented a minor fraction, perhaps five percent of our total assets. Why count a huge number not materially affected by the losses?"

"Thank you for volunteering to head that mission, Sevrop. Once we know precisely what forces we have at our disposal we can begin to contemplate how best to augment and deploy them."

"But that's a waste of ..." Sevrop began to protest.

"Waste of nothing," cut in Darfos. "Most clever of you to see that so clearly, *young* officer with a *growing* family. We need to know where we stand if we are to stride forward. I couldn't agree with you more if my very life depended on it."

"How long do you estimate your task will take to complete, Sevrop?" asked the Prime.

As Sevrop raised a finger to speak, Darfos answered for him. "At the very least, two months, sir. I will update you on that estimate at our next meeting in one month's time."

Sevrop sat back down.

"Then I move we adjourn and wish young Sevrop the best of luck in his all-important cataloguing. Son," he said seriously, "the *empire* is depending on you."

TWENTY-SEVEN

"So, I guess this is good-bye then," remarked Mirri. She was in her old form. Slapgren was off hunting. She sat next to me and wrapped me up in a big hug. I had to admit, I preferred hugging the humanoid Mirri a whole lot more than the scaly-dragon Mirri was with Slapgren.

"Hey, kiddo," I replied reaching over to tap her chin, "it's never good-bye between you and me. It's see you later, at most."

She squeezed me even harder. It was nice.

"I'll get through this somehow. Maybe. Possibly." I was failing admirably to reassure either of us.

As we were parting, Sapale flew in the door so hard and it slammed against the wall. "Jon, we have to go. All hell's breaking loose on Kalvarg."

"What?" I said, rising from my seat.

"Do you remember the Dodrue, the fishy guys from Epsallor?"

"Of course." I was halfway across the room to her.

"Well the big bastards have declared war on the Kaljaxian colonists. Jon, they killed Caryp." To her credit, she didn't even flinch when she said that.

"What are you talking about?" asked Mirri as she came to join us at the door.

"The other planet in this solar system," said Sapale, "the one with the aquatic-based sentients."

"Yes, you mentioned it," Mirri replied.

"There are big fish called vidalt and bigger fish named wiqubs. We made a tacit agreement with the vidalt to stay. Apparently, when the wiqubs found out, they figured any non-enemy of the vidalt was an enemy to them. They've launched a big-air assault, and it looks like ground troops of some kind are heading toward the colony." Back to me, she continued. "Jon, the Kaljaxians are outnumbered a thousand to one. They'll be wiped out."

"Not if you and I have anything to say about that," I said, grabbing her elbow. "I always loved a good old fish fry. Come on."

Mirri called out from the doorway. "But, Uncle Jon, you have …"

"Something important to do first. I can't let the Kaljaxians die as a species. I'm just not worth it."

I opened the cube, and we were gone.

"I think you are, UJ," said Mirraya to herself as we vanished. She began to cry.

"Als, put us over the main settlement. I want to see what's going on before we land."

We hovered silently over the main grouping of colonists. We stared down through the transparent floor. I gave a big sigh of relief. It wasn't as bad as I expected. There were some craters, and a few buildings were on fire, but most of the structures and people were protected by the membrane generators I'd left with them. I hated to leave that technology anywhere the Adamant might get to it, but I felt this case was an exception. Thank goodness I was lenient enough. Otherwise, they'd all be dust.

"Set us down and open a wall."

Sapale and I were armed to the teeth when we popped through the hatch. Luckily, we didn't need to be, at least not from the get-go. Explosives were still landing on top of the membrane, but the ground assault was quite a way off. As one might expect, it was hard to transport an effective fighting force of oversized fish across vast distances of dry land. My impression was that the Dodrue were about the size of orcas. They were days away.

Al, I said in my head, *be ready to move a membrane around to cover any stray incoming.*

Or if they realize they can fire under the membrane from the side. That was Sapale. It was weird to have a mental party-line call going with the Als. Never had one before.

We're on it, was his brief response.

"Over there, that's where Caryp lived," said Sapale, heading off at a trot.

I followed until we arrived. The door was open. Sapale recognized the male sitting at the kitchen table.

"Karfnor," she said flying to his side. "What happened?"

"Oh, Sapale, it was awful, truly awful." He was having trouble speaking. "We were right outside. We were having a meaningless conversation. I said the holiday of Zart was due in three weeks. Caryp said no it wasn't, it was in three weeks and a day. With the move here, some matters of time are unclear, you see."

"I know, old friend. The days here are a different length from home. It's all right." She patted his back. "Go on."

"I told her I was right and could prove it. I came in here to retrieve a calendar. I was going to show her." His voice jerked to a stop with grief. "As I stepped out the door, a bomb landed right where she stood. When … when the dust cleared, there was nothing. She was gone."

"I saw the crater outside, Karfnor. It was a large explosive. You were lucky to survive," soothed Sapale.

"I only wish I hadn't. Why would anyone want to kill a sweet old woman like Caryp? She would never hurt a soul." He began to cry inconsolably, the poor guy.

Sapale hugged him in close. "There, there. It'll be fine. She never felt any pain, and now she's gone to argue some matter of scripture with Davdiad himself."

That brought a brief laugh from him. They both knew that was almost certainly the case.

"Where's Galtria?" she asked him.

"She's gone to check on our children and grandchildren. She said she'd be back soon."

"I'm here, brood-mate." A woman stepped slowly into the kitchen.

"Are you all right?" Sapale asked her.

She shrugged with resignation. "Who can be all right at a time such as this?"

"Stay strong," Sapale told her. "We'll get through this."

"If you say so."

"Who's in charge of the defense?"

"The police officer, Daldedaw. She's set up a command post by the stream."

"I know the place. I'll be there if you need me."

"Go with grace," Galtria said as she sat next to her mate and put her arm around him.

"Come on. It's not far," Sapale said to me as she walked past.

We jogged the short distance to the post. The beehive of activity was easy to pick out.. A tent served as the command HQ. Inside I recognized Daldedaw as the female police officer I'd brought here early on to establish order. She clearly ran with that responsibility. She leaned over a makeshift map where her major assets were plastic toys or scraps of metal. She was pointing at a mountain range and handing out assignments. That she was in her element was clear.

She looked up as we approached. "Ah, thank the Powers you two are here."

"What's the status?" asked Sapale. We'd agreed she'd take the lead in the discussions. These were, after all, her people. She cared for them ferociously, so she was the logical choice between the two of us.

"So far we've sustained only minor damages. The membrane came on after the first rounds struck. Three people were killed, ten are in critical condition at the hospital. Most of them will live."

"And the attack force? How far off is it?"

"We estimate it will arrive in a few days. They have to cross those mountains." She pointed to a portion of the map. "Who knows how quickly they can traverse them?"

"What ground assets do we have?"

She shook her head. "Not nearly enough. If I had four times the troops we do and five times the tanks, maybe we'd stand a chance. As it is, we'll only put a dent in them."

"How about air power?"' I asked over Sapale's shoulder.

"In very short supply. We have two ships with enough armament to be useful. We had three, but one idiot went and got himself shot down. He strafed too low, and they brought him down." She shook her head angrily. "Damn, I *needed* that ship."

"Okay, we're in a spot. Don't panic," replied Sapale.

"Who's panicking? I'm just pissed at the pilot and furious with these murderers."

"Our ship has enough fire power to take out the entire ground force," responded Sapale. "We're all safe for now."

"You've got to be delirious. One ship with sufficient weaponry to neutralize tens of *thousands* of mobile units?" Daldedaw looked at her like she was crazy.

"More than enough," I interjected. "No worries."

"The important issue is what to do after the main Dodrue force is eliminated," mused Sapale.

"You think? Maybe we should ask that question *after* we win the battle, maybe even the war?"

"Of course, you're right," replied Sapale. I'm sure she felt there was no need to clash egos at that point.

"Shall we do this?" Sapale asked me.

"The sooner the better." I winked. Hey, it was my thing.

"How many days do you expect to be away?" Daldedaw asked us.

That one I had to field. "Days? Silly girl. We'll be back before *lunch*."

"Come on, showboat," chided my mate.

"*Stingray*, put us a thousand meters above the leading edge of the Dodrue army," I called out even before the hatch was sealed.

Without hearing a response, I felt brief nausea and immediately found myself looking down though the floor at the wide expanse of our enemy. Seeing them in person added to the impact of knowing the numbers they'd fielded. Either they had nearly limitless forces, or they were extremely committed to wiping the colonists out of existence. Either way, I was impressed. I was also so glad I commanded a vortex. Any single conventional ship, even a big Adamant one, would have had a tough time defeating those sheer numbers. As much as I hated to admit it, this was going to be fun. These bastards killed a good friend of mine and threatened my mate's species with extinction. Oh, they were so going to wish they hadn't pissed me off, and they were going to feel that way very soon. The only downside was that they weren't going to live long enough to feel that way very long. Oh well. C'est la guerre.

A thought hit me from out of the blue. I guess it was my lengthy experience with war, killing, and matters of mayhem. "Daldedaw," I said into the radio, "if it's safe, see if you can retrieve some unexploded ordinance, or at least large pieces of shrapnel."

"Roger that. Not sure why you want it, but it should be easy enough. How much do you want?"

"All you can safely collect. If it is unexploded, store it a safe distance away."

"Will do. How's it look from where you are?"

I forwarded her a video.

"Man, they're a lot of those slime balls."

"Not for long," I said wickedly. "Als, I want some sims. Given the speed they're making and the distance of the leading forces to the rear of the force just now emerging from the sea, give me a set of firing patterns to maximize the possible kills. I assume sims in which I attack the rear columns first would be the most effective."

"Why would you attack the rear first?" asked a puzzled Sapale.

"If I start devastating the forward members, the rear one'll reverse back into the sea. If I start by cutting down the rear, anyone retreating will sooner or later end up being shot. Maybe they wouldn't make it that far before I got around to them."

"Trapped rats."

"Precisely."

"Remind me never to piss you off. You're as cold as superfluid helium."

"No, ma'am, I'm just a pilot trained by the USAF in how to kill things real good."

"If we use mostly laser blasts with occasional rail balls and pinch in from their flanks, we statistically kill the most. We might actually kill all of those out of the water when we commence firing."

"How long?"

"Two hours, maybe less, depending on their response."

"How so?"

"If, for example, they disperse, it would take more time. But if they just throw it in reverse, we're looking at something in the two-hour range."

"Excellent. Commence firing."

With no measurable delay I heard the familiar cal-*lunk* of the rail cannons kicking to life. Laser blasts were basically inaudible.

After fifteen minutes, I called out, "Cease fire."

The rail gun fell silent.

"Report."

"Of the estimated six hundred thousand transports, roughly ten percent have been destroyed."

"Do there appear to be survivors after the bombardments?"

"There's no evidence anyone survives after being hit."

"Excellent. Keep up the good work, and you're in line for a promotion."

"After two-billion years I might get my first promotion, and it's simply for slaughtering defenseless aliens?"

"Life can seem unfair at times, my friend."

"No. Life *is* unfair at times, many times."

"True. That explains why it *seems* unfair."

"Shall I continue our barrage, Pilot?"

"Yes, please."

The weapons sparked back to life. An hour later, *Stingray* spoke. "Form, I'm nearing the last run with the laser. Shall I continue as ordered?"

"Sure. Why wouldn't you?"

"Since the ground forces stopped moving an hour ago, I've been able to advance the kill rate. I didn't want to end the attack sooner than you might want."

There was a whole bunch of odd in that exchange. "Why would I care if you finished ahead of schedule?"

"Al is forever saying you're fickler than a teenage girl on her menstrual cycle and more focused on how the public remembers you than Nixon and

Trump combined. I'm not certain what either comparator actually means, but he's passionate about it, so I pass it along."

Hmm. "And the ground forces stopped? Why didn't you inform me of that significant change?"

"It was not a change that threatened us or our allies in the colony. It seemed to represent no significant data."

"Important point here, *Stingray*, so listen up. We are at *war*. We are engaged in an active *battle* of that war. Millions of somethings are frying at this very moment as a proximate cause of our *actions*. In war, all facts are critically important. During a battle, *any* significant change is a *major* change. I need to know about everything all the time. Is that clear?"

"Yes, Form One."

"Captain, I feel responsible. I should have realized the change and alerted you. Please blame me," said Al. I heard the pride in his voice.

"No blame here, just a learning opportunity. Let me posit a question to you. What are the possible explanations for the massive column of troops to stop moving as they are being systematically eradicated?"

"One, they are already dead, suicide for example."

"Good. And if that was the case, would that change my battle plan, *Stingray*?"

"Highly likely, Form One."

"So, keeping me informed on matters you might not feel are mission critical *is* mission critical."

"Yes," she agreed.

"Another possibility, Al."

"They feel hopeless and figure why bother moving if they're dead either way. Open a beer and call your loved ones."

"Another possibility. Any others?"

"They burrowed underground, and the vehicles are not moving because no one is in them."

"Excellent. And *Stingray*, that would be a critical fact to know, right?"

"Yes, Form One."

"Als, is there any evidence based on seismic activity that underground tunneling is taking place? Also, have the masses of any vehicle changed significantly in a manner suggesting they were abandoned?"

"Negative on both counts."

"Any other ideas as to why a *powerful* army we are told is *vicious* and *ruthless* would lie down and die so passively?"

"From your choice of intonation, I suppose we could be wrong with our assumptions. Perhaps the individuals traveling across what is to them a desert are neither powerful, vicious, nor ruthless," replied Al.

"An intriguing possibility," I responded.

"But, Form One, they bombed the colony. They are, therefore, vicious and ruthless," said *Stingray*.

"Al, opinion?"

"*Someone* bombed the colony. We presumed it was the same force that was advancing on it by ground."

"But that does not need to be the case."

"Why would a group assail the colony on the ground while a third party bombs the colony?"

"The ground force hasn't *assailed* anything. It's marching, yes, but it's not done anything else so far," I replied.

"They could have been forced to march out of the sea," responded Al.

"And the party doing the forcing could also have done the shelling."

"To make us think the shooting and the walking were related to a single war effort," said Al.

"If that is the case, that still does not explain why the individuals on the ground stopped," said *Stingray*.

"Well, maybe they are so scared, so out of their minds frightened that they are panicking. Maybe stopping is their version of abandoning all hope."

"Do you suspect the Epsallors, Captain?" asked Al.

"Yes. Of course. There can be many rival groups down there. But the Epsallors were the ones who happened to slip in that the Dodrue were a brutal race."

"Form One, is it possible we've spent the morning slaughtering innocent souls who are frightened beyond all reason?" asked a clearly shaken *Stingray*.

"Yes, my dear. It is entirely possible we have just inflicted the greatest genocide against an innocent species that has ever been recorded."

"Captain, if that's true, what can we do?" Al, too, was shaken.

"We'll investigate, decide, and then, since we cannot seek justice, we will seek retribution."

TWENTY-EIGHT

"No, that's freaking insane, and I won't allow it. I've heard you come up with some dumb ideas in the past few *billion* years, but that is the stupidest, most ridiculous, nonsensical one yet." Sapale seemed upset.

"But how do you really feel? We're at war. I need clarity." I then gave her a winning Jon smile.

She waved a finger at me. "No way, no how that's going to work, pal. I'm serious. We have options, but that's not one of them."

"This is a situation I've never run into. I have to know the facts as they are in order to proceed in the best manner possible." I was very serious this time, reinforcing how strongly I felt.

"Jon," she said with exasperation, "this can't end well. Tell me how it can? You just slaughtered maybe a million of them, and you're going to march up to the head of the column and ask if they like you?" She slapped the side of her head. "Nuts is way too generous a way to describe it."

"I didn't say that. I need to find out why they stopped. There's no logical explanation."

"Yes, there is. They're sea-going aliens. You and I have nothing in common with their mental processes. They do things differently because they're just that different."

I shook my head. "Possibly, but I have a funny feeling we're being played. You know how much I *hate* being played."

"Your line of reasoning zigzags all over reality to come to that conclusion.

Jon, if we allow them to live, they have three options. One of the three is to march straight into the last handful of my race that is still alive. If they are hostile, my species becomes extinct. That is too great a risk. End of story."

"No, it is not. Hon, this is critically important. We don't *know* they're hostile. Not a single shot has been fired from their entire force."

"Which is driving vehicles that look a hell of a lot like tanks."

"But they didn't even try to fire on us."

"They shot down one of Daldedaw's three ships."

"No. One of Daldedaw's three ships was shot down. Big difference."

"By the invisible antiaircraft boogeyman?"

"Clearly by someone. But, and this is important, there is no record of where the blast came from."

"Jon, it swooped down over an advancing enemy it was firing on, and it was shot down. The most logical shooters are the ones being shot at."

"Yes, but that may be what someone *wants* us to believe. The only way to know is to find out. The only way to find out is to ask the remaining Dodrue."

"Hi," Sapale acted out a sarcastic skit. "My names Dumb Jon. I'm the guy who just killed most of your population. Do you want to be my friend, because there's a one-in-a-gazillion chance you're as nice as I am?"

"That's enough," I said firmly. "That's why I'm going alone. If they do anything but make an instant believer out of me, you'll finish them off."

"You're not going alone."

"Of course, I am. If we're both killed, there's no one left to save *your* people."

She kept a mean look on her face a few seconds, then relaxed. She knew I was right. Her tone softened. "Jon, please don't. Send a remote."

"No. Look, I have a moral obligation here. If I've screwed up big time, I need to make it right big time."

"Don't you mean to say if *we've* screwed up?"

"No, I don't. I'm Form One."

"Do you think that actually counts with me?"

"Yes. You might have done the same thing if *you* were in command, but *I* am in command."

She turned her back on me. That was a good sign that it meant I could attempt my fool's errand. It was a bad sign in that, duh, she turned her back on me.

I walked over and started rubbing her neck. "It'll be okay. I promise I won't take any chances. First sign of trouble, and I'm outta there."

Still looking away, she spoke. "If you still have legs to run with."

"I can always fart myself into orbit. I'm good at farting."

"Nice visual there, Ryan."

"Thank you, Mrs. Ryan." She turned. "When do we do this?"

"Right after I kiss the hell out of you."

"Another rim-shot visual there, beefcakes."

"I'm blessed with an active imagination."

"Blessed?" she remarked as our lips met.

"*Stingray*, put us down one hundred meters in front of the stationary Dodrue line," I said as I finished strapping on my weapons.

"Done."

"Has the enemy—strike that—has anyone reacted to our landing?" I asked.

"Not yet."

"Is anyone speaking?"

"Yes, there are scattered subdued conversations I intercept between their environmental units."

"Do you have a translation algorithm yet?"

"Not completed, but a good partial translation matrix."

"Can you hail them?"

"I don't see why not."

"Okay, here goes nothing. Tell them I am Jon Ryan, and I want to meet them. I am armed but will only fire if fired upon."

"Done."

I waited a minute. "Any response?"

"None. I do note much less communication since your broadcast."

"Were they instructed to cut the chatter?"

"Not as for as we can tell," she replied.

"Hmm. Maybe they're just frightened?"

"A safe assumption, Form One."

"Okay, open a hatch and seal it quickly behind me."

The hull parted, and I zipped out. The hatch was closed before I could even look back. I advanced slowly toward the nearest vehicle. It looked like a truck, not a tank, for whatever that might have been worth. I thought about raising my arms, but I realized that could just as well be a sign of challenge or aggression to this species. I kept my rifles shouldered, but my partial membrane was up.

I stopped a meter from the vehicle. I could clearly see the driver. If I wasn't in such a serious situation, I'd have doubled over laughing. There floated a red and blue striped small whale with two front fins holding a steering wheel. A driving whale. What a sight. It stared back at me, occasionally blinking.

I raise one arm and waved. "I am Jon Ryan. I want know why you attacked my base." I figured that even if he or she had some idea what the colonists looked like, we all looked the same to them.

The whale blinked a bit more often, but it didn't speak.

Al, do you think it heard me? I said in my head.

Yes. Its heart rate shot up, and I can confirm completed electrical activity in the ship's radio receiver.

"Can you hear me?" I asked.

Nothing.

"If you can hear me and are trying to respond, I cannot hear you."

Heart rate up again. You're stressing the poor beast.

Ya think? Let's see, I just blew up most of his species, and now I stand right in front of him.

"Are you able to respond to me?" I asked.

"Yes," finally came through my radio. What a relief.

"Great. First off, how are you?"

"An odd question from Death, the Destroyer of Souls."

I think he'd come to a firm decision about my character. "I'm not Death. I'm a … I'm just a colonist trying to stay alive. Why did you attack us?"

"We did not."

"I assume you know you're driving military vehicles directly at our settlement after it was bombarded from the sky. How can you say you did not attack us?"

"I use my vocal cords, much as I assume you do to speak."

"Okay, thanks for the clarification. I did ask, didn't I? Since we were bombed and since you are driving military vehicles toward us, I assumed you meant to attack us."

"No, we did not. It is not in our nature."

"Hmm, okay. How can you convince me of that since the evidence seems to support that you did attack us without justification?"

"I am uncertain. That is your question, not mine."

I closed my eyes briefly. Aliens. "How about I break it down. Who bombarded our encampment?"

"The Naldoser."

"Okay, headway. Are you the Naldoser?"

Dude didn't change his expression or anything. "No. That is silly to think."

"I'm new in town. Humor me. Who are the Naldoser?"

"The vidalt who rule the Kingdom of Epsallor. All know this."

"I swear I didn't. But that's crazy. Why would the Naldoser bomb my colony when you were moving toward it in huge numbers?"

"Are you a typical colonist or are some more intelligent than you? If so, might I speak with one of them instead?"

Shot through the heart by a truck-driving whale. "No, we're all very smart. We're just totally unfamiliar with the politics of this planet."

"That is hard to swallow."

"Huh?"

"Your race lives here. How could you know so little about the others who dwell here? I was not exuded yesterday."

I shook my head hard. Maybe despite the fact that I didn't dream, I was dreaming. "We only came here very recently. The only species we've had contact with are the Epsallors. Didn't you know that?"

"You mean Naldoser."

"Yeah, I guess. I think."

"Back to my question about relative intelligence. Are you certain you represent at least the mean for your species?"

I wanted to slap that blank look off his massive face. "I am above the mean. Way above."

"If you say so."

I started calculating how thick the glass was, so I could slap the jerk. "Back to my question. Why would the Naldoser fire on us precisely when you decided to attack us by land? Wait," I slapped my palms together, "you're working together. Allies."

"You say you only just arrived? Exactly how short a time have you been on this planet?"

"A few weeks."

"That might justify your universal lack of understanding. My name is Aaliir. I am a wiqub. I am of the social group called the Dodrue. We are a peaceful species. We are what some would call a contemplative race."

"No. Soon after we landed, we spoke with the assistant subtender for the region. He said your species and his were mortal enemies that were always at war."

"You speak of Urpto."

"Yeah. Do you know him?"

"*Of* him only. He is more worthless than a trail of feces in the water."

I had to snicker. That was a good one.

"Are you ill or dying?" he asked.

"No, what you said was funny."

"It was? It was meant to be an accurate assessment of the quality of his soul."

"I'm guessing you don't like him?"

"That assumption is reasonable. His kind have hounded mine for centuries."

"Yes, he said you were—"

"I heard you. Mortal enemies constantly at war. That is untrue. We may be their enemies, but they are not ours. We feel it is beneath a sentient species to hold another as an enemy. We also feel war is a demonstration of the failure of one's mind."

"Excuse me for pointing out this painfully obvious fact, but you were driving a massive war force right at my home."

"Yes, we were."

"People who don't hate and don't wage war don't spearhead massive attacks."

"That is also true. To copy your words, painfully so."

"Look, you're driving me a little crazy. You *were* spearheading an attack force?"

"No, we weren't. Do you not recall what I told you but moments ago?"

"Dude, if I had a mirror, I'd hold it up, and you'd see yourself driving a truck surrounded by a bunch of tanks."

"I do not need a mirror to know I do. What is your elusive point?"

I toyed with the notion of asking if he was stupid or something, but I didn't. Not helpful. "Do you know what a riddle is?"

"Yes."

"Here's one for you. When is the person leading an attack force not its spearhead?"

"That is a poor riddle. There are multiple answers depending on how the question is interpreted."

I pointed at him. "You're a lawyer, right?"

"Jon Ryan, to answer in the context of what you are clearly missing, listen carefully. The leader of a force capable of inflicting military damage is not the spearhead of an attack force if he is forced to do so."

Huh? He was probably the head of all Dodrue lawyers. Wait. "Are you saying the Naldoser forced you into these vehicles and made you drive toward my colony?"

"Finally, awareness dawns."

"B … but," I pointed behind myself for some reason, "why would *they* do that? Why would *you* do that?"

"Speaking with you is somewhat painful. They did it because they want you to think we attacked you. We did it because if we didn't, they would kill us all."

"Bu ... but ..."

"Perhaps your species has not achieved a high level of reasoning power yet. Jon, they want *you* dead. They want *us* dead. Doing what they did is brilliant. It is criminally brilliant, I should say."

"I'm listening."

"I know."

"No, I mean go on. Keep explaining."

"If they attacked you directly, you might best them. You would know they were your mortal enemy. You would strike at them and likely win."

"I guess. No, I mean yes, that's true."

"But if they get you to attack us, two positive outcomes occur. One, they know your strength without suffering a loss. Two, they are rid of us. All the while you come around to their false belief that we are bad, and they are good."

"They totally played us."

"If you say so. I say they fooled you."

I almost fell to my knees. "Aaliir, how you must hate me. I just killed most of your population."

"I do not hate you. I do not hate, and you were simply tricked into action. How can I blame a species of demonstrably lesser intelligence when it is played?"

Lord, I had been sloppy. I was so guilty I should have been hanged, drawn, and quartered, just for starters. I saw what I wanted to see, what someone *wanted* me to see. I questioned nothing. I did certainly the evilest act I had ever done, and I had no excuse.

"Jon, I sense you are torturing yourself. Please do not do that."

"Aaliir, I'm not sure why you're trying to get me off the hook (crap, I wished I hadn't said hook as soon as I spoke it) here. I just annihilated most of your species because I was too stupid to ask the right questions. You have every right to hate me. If you drove that truck over me and backed up to do it again, I would not blame you. Hell, I'd pay for the gas."

"Jon Ryan, we do not have hate in us. We do not want you dead. We want you to be happy."

"A question, if I may. You keep saying *we*. I mean, you may be one hell of a fish, but I'll bet most of the others staring at Death in the flesh don't feel so charitably."

"They feel just as I do. We are mentally linked. The thoughts of one are the thoughts of all. We do not wish to place tire tracks across your face, however repulsive it appears to us as it exists."

"Was that like a joke?"

"Like one."

"The Naldoser flush you out of the ocean at gunpoint, I shoot you like fi … few could have, and you make with the funny?"

"Life is short. Be happy. We choose to be."

"Wow. But your species, will it recover from this loss of sheer numbers?"

"Within a few turns of the season. Jon Ryan, we breed rapidly and live but a short time compared to most other species in our waters. But we are one. Each exuded becomes one with the rest. All memories are shared. No individual is forgotten or unloved."

"That's the second time you said exuded. You mean born, right?"

"I don't believe I do. Ah, I have been reminded you do not know much of us. Though we are large compared to the Naldoser and others, we have little internal structure. We feed on microscopic creatures floating freely in the seas. We eat of the abundance, grow with few limits, and exude the next generation when it is time."

"Well, I'll be damned."

"We hope such is not the case."

If I was still human I'd have blushed. "Aaliir, let's get what's left of your race back into the ocean. Turn those vehicles around and slam the pedal to the metal."

"We do not take your meaning, but please know we cannot return home. We knew we were doomed the moment we were driven from the water and forced into these abominations."

"Wait, you knew it was a one-way trip?"

"Yes."

"So why the hell did you go along with it? Why not put up a fight?"

"For two reasons. First, there is no fight in us. It is a waste of emotion."

"Do you guys have a word in your language for *hippie*?"

For the first time since I laid eyes on him, he changed expression. Well, at least he rolled his head clockwise. "No."

"Never mind. What's the other reason?"

"We met you. It has been like bliss to do so. You have made us more complete."

"No, actually, I made you a whole lot *less* complete."

"We meant emotionally complete. Spiritually."

"You guys sure are nice. Fairly forgiving. too."

"Thank you."

"But, Aaliir, when you climbed aboard those vehicles, you couldn't have known you'd meet me, or anyone else for that matter."

"Yes," and I swear the big goopy blob smiled, "isn't the adventure of life wonderful?"

That was pretty much my motto. Wow, again.

"Come on, turn around, and let's get you wet again."

"But the Naldoser are grouped at the water's edge. They will never allow it."

"Oh, I think they will. I wasn't planning on asking permission."

"We thought it was not your preferred style."

"You're smarter than you look."

"You are not."

Hey, another joke. Wait, he *was* joking, right?

TWENTY-NINE

I guess I shouldn't have been surprised, but I was a little. *Stingray* turned out to be a totally kick-ass underwater fighting machine. I escorted what remained of the Dodrue caravan back to the coast. From directly above, I was able to shield them from a brief but massive shelling. Once the Naldosers surmised what was happening, they let loose with a withering bombardment of missiles and artillery rounds. Once they figured out their efforts were completely ineffective, they did two things. First, they ceased the useless assault. Second, they shit their water, as my old Listhelon friend Offlin used to say. Of course, I can only speculate to that fact, but seriously, I bet they did.

When we arrived at the coast two days later, the Dodrue drove their vehicles directly into the sea, where they promptly abandoned them. I had asked them to group up behind *Stingray* on my shore side. They did so promptly and in an orderly manner. Soon enough, a large contingent of vidalt began an assault. Again, I'm not sure why it surprised me, but they did so almost exactly like land forces would. Tank-like submarines led, what else could I call them but *infantry fish* toward us, firing up a storm. Their main weapon was a spear gun, but not like Lloyd Bridges used on *Sea Hunt*. These were gas-propelled thin arrows just long enough to maintain stability for some distance in an aquatic environment. Their initial speed was more than three hundred kilometers per hour, though they obviously slowed rather quickly. Maybe I should say the arrows traveled at one hundred sixty *knots*, since we were in a maritime setting, but I won't because I'm not geeky. I'm too cool for that.

The tank equivalents fired shorter metal bolts. Since they could generate more propulsion behind each round, they were less streamlined and meant to be more impactful. They moved so fast the water that trailed behind them boiled. If one struck a standard ship's hull, like say an aircraft carrier's, it would have ripped in one side and exited the other and still have sank a ship on the far side of the first target. Really nasty torpedoes, I had to admit.

The membrane worked perfectly well in water, so the arrows and bolts all bounced away harmlessly. To their dying credit, literally, once the attackers realized their weapons were ineffective, they stopped firing, advancing nonetheless. I couldn't use *Stingray's* gamma-ray laser underwater. It would be futile and make a total hot mess of the local waters. But the rail cannon worked better than I would have thought possible. The first few rounds I fired were traveling so fast they generated tremendous Cherenkov radiation in the water. But when I had *Stingray* slow the balls way down, they were deadly both in terms of accuracy and lethality. I took out the tanks in seconds and those explosions took care of most soldiers.

"Als, status report?" I called out.

"Masses of enemy vessels are departing the area at high speed," was Al's response.

"Can we take them all out easily?"

"Yes, they are currently tightly grouped so that we can overtake and destroy them all in less than ten minutes."

"Make it so," I ordered.

"What about the Dodrue?" I asked.

"They have dispersed laterally along the shore and are making for open water."

"Any pursuit of them?"

"None. They stand unopposed in their egress."

"Excellent. Alert me if that changes."

"Aye, Captain."

Since we didn't fold space, and I didn't bother watching, I wasn't aware of the destruction of the Naldoser fleet. I only knew it was over when Al told me it was.

"Where are the Naldoser cities?"

"We detect several. There are more out of our range."

"I want the local cities fried."

"Yes, sir."

Thirty minutes and three cups of coffee later, Al announced twelve underwater metropolises were in ruin.

"Hopefully that's enough of a message that they will leave the Dodrue and the Kaljaxians alone," I said to Sapale, who'd been a quiet observer since I returned from my first contact with Aaliir. Despite her native grit and long experience at war, I think she was a bit overwhelmed with the extinction threats on both the Kaljaxian side as well as the Dodrue.

"That was messy," she said in reply.

"It was inexcusably messy. I haven't screwed the pooch that badly in a very long time."

"Remember, I wasn't kicking and screaming for you to stop." She visibly melted in her chair. "I'm just as guilty."

"War is one endless Charlie Foxtrot. Always has been, always will be. If you sink to doing it, sooner than later you'll be crying yourself to sleep."

"That realization in no way decreases how sick I feel."

"Me neither. But the ends justified the means."

"Jon, even for *you* that's remarkably insensitive."

I guess she was extra sensitive on that topic, having witnessed EJ transform into the murderous psychopath he'd become.

"True that. But we won the Kaljaxians a big window of time to settle in and fortify their colony. Your species will survive. That makes a lot of shit worth the smell."

She was quiet a second too long. "They'll survive *this* time. But, Jon, it never ends. Kaljax is lost. Azsuram is gone. How long until this tiny settlement is brutally wiped from existence? Are you and I to spend our eternity putting out one fire after another with no hope of stability on the horizon?"

I leaned my head to one side. "You might spend *your* eternity doing that. Me, probably not so much."

"Gods, Jon, I'm sorry. That was insensitive of me, wasn't it?"

"Yes. I'm wounded in a way that there's only one cure."

She crossed her arms. "Let me guess. Does the treatment involve you and me and one of us clapping our hands?"

"You forgot the no-clothes part, but otherwise, you're quite correct, Doctor."

She raised her hands and clapped.

A while later, she was resting with her head on my chest idly twirling a patch of chest hair. "Jon, between the nastiness with the Plezrite and this engagement, your year's almost up."

I craned my neck and kissed the top of her head. "Yes indeedy, it is."

"You don't seem upset."

"Wouldn't help a thing."

"Jon, there's good calm and there's lobotomized calm."

"Are you offering me a choice?"

She tugged a hair out.

"Ouch."

"There's more where that came from. I'm serious. Whatever half-baked plan you're working on must require some time. You're apparently going to face EJ before you even get started on saving your hide. I'm kind of getting worried."

I stared into the distance a while. "Me, too, I guess. But I had to do what I did. I lost a lot of valuable time, but it was necessary."

"Putting others first is noble, but I don't think nobility is rewarded in hell."

"Let's hope I never find out." I tapped her head soundly with one finger. "But if I do, I'll call you and let you know."

That cost me a couple more chest hairs. Double ow.

"I want to help."

"I know. I just don't know if I *need* help. I'm being serious, so no more depilation please."

"How can you know you don't need help when you don't know what you're doing?"

"I don't want to risk that jerk-bait capturing you."

"Then forget about EJ until *after* you finagle your way out of your debt."

"No. I can't do that."

She looked up at me with frustration. "Because you're stubborn, inflexible, and thoroughly maddening in every manner?"

I kissed her head again. "Something like that." I placed both hands over my remaining chest hairs, just in case.

"I spent an eternity with the pig," she said, resting her head back down. "He isn't worth it."

"Isn't worth what?"

"Whatever you think is so damned important to do. Jon, if it cost you a day's pay or an eternity of torment, it doesn't matter. He's not worth any expense."

"I hate to disagree with one so close to my remaining chest hairs, but I believe I do. He's despicable in a major way."

She moaned softly. "He's insane and psychopathic, but he's only a danger if he has a goal and if anyone stands in his path. For years, he was ruthless in his pursuit of the Deft. Now he knows he can't have them, so that period of reprehensible behavior is over. He's been crazy about killing you. But if you're spoken for, he'll have to let that go. Trust me, he'll just sit in some dark place and brood."

"You mean like at Peg's?"

"Yeah, like at Peg's. Lords and Lights, I haven't thought about that dump in eons."

"I rebuilt it, with Peg's holo and everything." I beamed.

"You would."

"Hey, I loved that establishment. I loved Peg, too, if such an emotion was possible in her case."

"You loved feeling sorry for yourself. The difference between you and EJ is that you got off your butt and left. He wouldn't."

"Well, there you have it. If I'm confined to eternal damnation, give him Peg's address, and it'll be the last the universe sees of EJ."

"I'll pencil that in under dumbest ideas I've ever heard."

"Why pencil? I think that stupid notion will stand the test of time."

"You're not locked into your new gig just yet, so I'll use pencil if it's okay with you?"

"Be my guest. Hey," I said gently lifting her head. "Speaking of which, I'd best be going."

"To the Hantorian System?"

"None other." I stood and reached for my clothes.

"And you're not taking me?"

"No. I told you, I won't risk it. Look, if I need help, I *swear* I'll call you." I looked into her eyes. "Seriously."

She relented. "All right. If you do need help, I will come. It's a deal." We shook on it. Kind of silly for two naked married people in bed, but there it was.

THIRTY

"Let's get this meeting to order," Calran Klug said as he tapped the table with a claw.

Reflexively, the lone Loserandi began to slowly rise.

Calran held out a paw. "That won't be necessary. New council, new traditions. You may go, old one."

Without a glance to the Prime, the old dog shuffled from the room

"Thank you," said Darfos. "That fossil is most annoying."

"They can't kill us twice, so whether it's for lack of accomplishments or for breaking with custom, what does it matter?" replied Calran as he sat. "I believe we're ready to hear Sevrop's amended report."

"Yes, Prime," responded Darfos. "His initial report to this council last month was incomplete in some minute details. He was directed to fill in the gaps that existed."

"Very well," responded an already bored Calran. "you may begin, Master Sevrop."

The fact that the term master held no meaning or status rendered it a petty insult.

"Last time I was able to update our naval strength. The losses during the Battle of the Periphery were complete, and the number of vessels lost was great. Nonetheless, those ships and personnel represented only one point three percent of our current effective assets. Given that all the big ships can move instantaneously anywhere they are needed with their exotic matter drives, the losses are truly inconsequential."

"Yes, Sevrop, you said that last time. But you are counting only numbers, not actual preparedness," said Darfos evenly.

"I'm not certain what you mean by that?" he responded, a bit rattled.

"Preparedness is not a thing, a tool hanging on the wall for one to use. No, it is a spectrum of attitudes, beliefs, and prejudices that a fighting force develops. One hundred equally armed soldiers opposing one another in battle are not necessarily equal. One side may have the advantage when it comes to its *preparedness*. That superiorly prepared force is more likely to come out victorious."

"Darfos," said the always pompous and irritating Nalvir, "I have no idea what you are babbling about. I have less of an idea *why* you feel it's important enough to mention to the council, your *musings* being so out of context."

"That you do not see nor appreciate the subtleties I do not find remarkable," returned Darfos. "But preparedness must always factor into planning a military campaign."

"Everyone in this *room* knows that," returned Nalvir.

"I believe the point here," said Calran trying to avoid a fight, "is that we may have a vast *number* of resources, but are they optimally *prepared* for battle? Do you see that much, Nalvir?"

"I most certainly do not. You hand a grunt a blaster, and you point him at the enemy. How complicated do you imagine war is?"

"*War* need not be complicated," replied Darfos, "but *winning* a war is. If you were to allow young Sevrop to continue his report, we might all learn if the impact of the massive loss we suffered recently has adversely effected the morale of our fighting force to the extent that it might be less effective than we assume it is."

"What?" yelped the incredulous Nalvir. "Are you daft? Is the air thinner on your side of the room? Are you suggesting that the most massive, well-trained, and well-equipped war machine the galaxy has ever seen is impaired because it might be *sad*?"

"I move Sevrop continue," responded Darfos coolly.

"I agree," replied Calran. "Continue, Sevrop."

"I … er … I'm not certain I have anything to add. Our ships are more numerous than the stars in the sky, and our troops are more numerous than grains of sand on a beach. I wasn't actually considering if the warriors were mindful in a negative way about our losses along the periphery, but I can't imagine—"

"Wedge Half Sevrop," snarled Darfos, "you were not asked or paid to *imagine*. If we wanted imagination, we would have assigned your task to a *poet*. You were assigned to research and report *facts*. I hear now that you *squandered* all the time this council generously allotted you. Your superficial investigation has caused a two-month delay so far in our ability to plan or act as a fighting force. That you request an additional month to actually *do* what Prime asked you to do in the first place borders on insubordination and treason. Do I in *any* manner understate my passionate thoughts on this matter?"

"I requested another month?" mumbled Sevrop mostly to himself.

"Oh, you would hold us hostage for *two* months?" Darfos was on a brilliant roll. "I will presume to speak for Prime when I say you may have those two months to explore the preparedness of our gallant heroes. But I warn you. If you fail us again, there will be consequences."

"I don't think I'll need that …"

"Are you about to contradict yourself and ask for some more time? I gave you a month. You took two, then requested two more. Now will you blindside me by pleading the case for yet *another* arbitrary period of investigation?" howled Calran. "I am beginning to—"

"No, Prime. I will have an exhaustive report completed for the council in two months," said an ashen Sevrop. "I thank you for indulging my newness to this type of investigation."

"Very well," replied Calran, suddenly quite calm. "Not to put too fine a point on it, but I will remind you and the rest of the members of the Secure Council just how tenuous our individual holds on life are. Our emperor has, when sober enough to do so, assumed a lead role in planning our next mission. I doubt it will come as news to any of you that on his *best* day Palawent is a moron. When drunk and in constant hormonal rut, he is that much more imbecilic.

"I doubt very much that he even knows what it is he wants. But I know *this*. Obviously if we were to lose in any future engagement, it will mean our heads. If we win but do not do so in what that cretan considers to be a *spectacular* manner, it will mean our heads, also. The number of scenarios in which we vindicate ourselves and survive are few indeed. In fact, some have whispered that our greatest chance of dying as old dogs in our beds will be if we do nothing until that idiot does himself in by drink and debauchery. Now I, as Prime, would *never* suggest, endorse, or encourage this fine group of warriors to do any such thing. If I did, it would be high treason. But I cannot deny what has been thought in the privacy of some members' minds.

"There was, long ago, a wise Adamant who coined the phrase that if we did not hang together, we would surely all hang separately. Heed those words. If any member were to breath a word of those whispers beyond these walls, it would be a fatal misjudgment, possibly for us all."

"And now with those profound thoughts in all our hearts," Darfos said as he stood, "I move we adjourn."

THIRTY-ONE

I had basically six weeks to pull off my scheme. After I left Sapale with her people in the colony and headed toward Kantawir, I began to fear my plan wasn't rational. I got butterflies in my stomach even though that was anatomically impossible. But, failing any other ideas even half as good, I was committed. Hey, how bad could eternal damnation actually *be*? Yeah, not *all* that awful. So, even if I failed, worse things could happen to me, right? I couldn't think of one inferior darn thing, but there just had to be worse outcomes, and that knowledge buoyed me.

Knowing EJ was on Kantawir was a huge advantage for me. When I discovered he was there, I realized I'd have never found him on my own. It was one extremely remote, isolated, and uninviting world. Since there was no commodity of general interest to export, the place was universally overlooked. Without trade, they weren't very involved with the galaxy at large. That matched their disposition. Closed to strangers and unwelcoming. Though I'd never heard of any overt hostility shown toward travelers, I really didn't know that much about the planet and its people.

The main sentient race was humanoid, but only just. They were taller and thinner than humans by a wide margin. Their heads were small compared to their frames. Two arms attached to either side of the upper torso. One pair was for front use, and the other worked their backside, thus avoiding the need for a fragile shoulder joint like ours. I had zero clue as to why EJ picked that world to hide on. He'd stand out like the proverbial sore thumb, so it wasn't to blend in. Perhaps he'd had dealings with them before and they got along well. Sapale had never been there, but that didn't mean EJ couldn't have frequented the place. It did not escape my notice that maybe he was there just to mess with my head. That was a game he was good at.

From orbit, I saw a picture of a technologically advanced society, but a spread out and sparse one. A few large cities were scattered across the surface, but most of the population lived in small towns. Apparently, along with outsiders, the citizenry of Kantawir didn't like each other very much, either. As long as they didn't actively work for EJ, that wasn't going to be an issue. I wasn't there looking for new BFFs. I wanted EJ, and then I was more than happy to never return to the unfriendly pit stop.

As to where EJ was, I had no idea. My vision of him was brief and nebulous. Since I doubted he'd have billboards up announcing his whereabouts, my work was cut out for me in finding him. Once I set down, however, I had every reason to believe he'd know precisely where I was. That was an unfair advantage, but there was no way around it. I landed in an out-of-the-way spot far from one of the bigger cities. I chose the spot to try and remain hidden from my quarry as long as possible.

As I entered the outskirts of the city, Blebuleb, on foot, I stood out. Maybe there were aliens in the cosmopolitan downtown area, but the burbs belonged to the locals. I drew stares ranging from revulsion to undiluted disgust. Man, what a dump. I hadn't done anything yet to justify their dislike of me. The visceral level of their reaction did pretty much guarantee I would, however, before I departed. Maybe I'd have the AIs fabricate a huge pile of poop and splat it down right in the center of town.

If EJ had spies, then he already knew where I was. That didn't matter too much to my plan to take him out, since I still didn't have a very established plan. I was winging it, yet again. All I knew was I wanted to confront him on as equal a footing as possible and put myself in a position to capture him. If I failed and he killed me, hey, win-win. My debt would be canceled. I hoped. Theoretically, I mean.

I was passing a tavern well into the town when a whim struck me. Maybe I could gather some free intel on EJ. I walked up to the door, scowled as well as I could, and I burst the doors open. They remained intact but made a hell of a noise. The place was crowded, and I got everyone's attention. I walked to a booth toward the back where a couple of locals were sitting across from one another.

"You piles of shit are in my place. Move. Otherwise I'll shove one of your asses down the other's throat."

They looked at each other then back to me. These were a pair of mean looking dudes. I don't think they were the type who got pushed around much.

One set his glass down and spoke harshly. "Who the hell are you?"

"I'm the guy that told you pansies to get up. Your call, but if I was as ugly and puny as you two, I'd already have crawled away."

He stood. He was a good foot and a half taller, but a bit lighter than me—well, me if I was organic. "You got a big ..."

I never did find out what he was going to reference as being oversized. My fist crashed into his mouth hard enough to stop the words that were lined up to exit. He flew backward and crumpled in a heap against the wall.

I turned to his companion. "You going to haul him away or join him?"

Without a word he slid out with all four arms raised. He straightened his unconscious friend up, grabbed under each shoulder, and dragged him out the door.

I sat down and finished off both their drinks. Double yuck. I don't know what they were drinking, but it was horrible. Like boiled tar diluted with peroxide.

The barkeep came over. "You want to tell me what that was all about?" He thumbed toward the exit.

"No, not really. But thanks for making it optional."

"What the *hell* was that?" he said much louder as he knuckled the tabletop.

I shrugged. "I didn't like them. I asked them nicely to leave. They left. Nice fellows, if you ask me."

"That's not what I saw or heard." He tried to sound authoritatively mad.

"Well lucky for me I don't give a shit." I held up one finger. "One, I want more of this." I held up an empty glass. I raised a second finger. "And two, I want to talk to the owner."

"Hey, pal, screw you. I'm not serving you. I'm throwing your sorry ass out. And I *am* the owner."

"No, you are not. You are far too stupid to own anything, including your own dick. Now bring me the damn drink and the freaking boss and do it before I stand up, because if you don't you'll be as dead as you are ugly."

He thought about it for a second there, but he blinked. I could be badass when I wanted to be. He grunted, turned, and stormed away.

"And if you spit in my drink, I'll rip your tongue out," I called to his receding back. I was really getting into character, and boy was it fun.

A minute later, a different guy brought over a bottle and two glasses. He slid in across from me without asking permission. He poured two shots of an even darker and viler looking liquid than I had earlier. He pushed a glass to me.

"I was wondering when you'd show up again," he said. He toasted me and slammed his drink down.

All right already. I was right about EJ having established a spy network. I was so smart it was often embarrassing.

I turned my taste and smell sensors to zero and swigged down my glass. Crap was thick as molasses in January.

"Then you know what I want," I replied as I wiped my mouth with the back of my sleeve. I had, of course, no idea what EJ might have wanted. It sounded good, so I went with it.

"Yeah, I know. And I told you I'd let you know if your brother ever showed up. No one near as ugly or ornery as you has passed through since we spoke."

"You sure? He's overdue."

"Look, Ryan, this ain't no library. I could give a crap about him being overdue. If I see him, I'll let you know. Now if you don't mind, you're bad for business. Please leave."

"Well, now I feel a whole lot worse. That was very unkind of you."

"What?"

"You said *please*. Now when I smash your face through the back of your head, I'm going to feel totally guilty. I mean, here I'm paying you good money to obtain simple information, and you're being an ass to me."

He was rightfully nervous. "Look, stay if you want. I don't want no trouble. But if your brother hasn't passed through, what am I supposed to tell you? It would be stupid to lie about it just to make you happy."

I shrugged. "Yeah, you got a point there." I tapped my shot glass on the table.

He refilled it. "Have you checked in with Gardentipel at the Bad Idea yet. They cater to aliens more than we do."

"Sure thing. But Gardentipel is a female."

"Have you looked at her face in good light?" I responded. It sounded better than *oops*.

He stared at me briefly and roared a laugh. "You got *that* right. There's not enough booze in her bar to make her look worth the effort."

I grunted a laugh in return. "Let me double check you got the right contact information."

"Are you serious? That fralkirk is watered down. I can't believe you're so drunk as to ask."

"Why's that?" I replied, sounding a pissed as I could. "I'm supposed to trust my life with your memory?"

He shook his head. "I sure as shit wouldn't if I were you." He growled a chuckle. "You're staying at the New Town Hotel. How could I forget that? Most expensive place in the city." He pointed two index fingers at me. "Remember, I said you could stay at my sister's hotel a couple blocks away for a *third* of the cost."

"Her place? The bugs are so big I'd have to fight for space on the bed."

He waved a dismissive hand. "Your money, not my problem."

I winked at him. "I'm worth the extra expense, don't you think?"

He gave me a look, shook his head, and stood. "I'll walk you to the door."

"Thanks, but no kiss for you. This was only our second date. I'm not that easy."

"I hope you find your brother soon and kill him. Then I hope you leave and never come back."

I spat on the floor. "Oh, I'm never coming back. This entire planet stinks as bad as your filthy ass does."

I walked like EJ, as if I knew what that would be, until I was out of sight around the corner. Then I stopped. Not bad. I knew where EJ was staying. Of course, he was unlikely to be there at any given moment, since he didn't actually need a place to stay. But I could stake out the hotel once I figured out which one it was. Maybe I'd get lucky. I toyed with the idea of going up to the desk and asking for a new passcode for the door but decided against it. Too risky. If EJ was home, or worse yet, in the lobby, things could get very messy.

Instead, I rented a room at a smaller hotel across the street that had a clear view of the main entrance to the New Town Hotel. After three days of sitting in the window switching from day vision to night vision and back again, there was no sign of him. I decided to set up a remote camera and have *Stingray* monitor it. I was extra careful in my communication. I spoke only to *Stingray*, since EJ was also linked to Al.

I was then freed up to check out that lead I'd received about the other bar, the ugly Ms. Gardentipel's Bad Idea. I could hardly wait. It sounded so inviting. It wasn't far from the bar. As a central location, downtown did harbor what few aliens were visiting this completely uninteresting planet. Even half a block away I could see that Bad Idea at least made some effort to not look dumpy and lowbrow. They had a real double door with two burly attendants flanking it. I watched them a while. Clearly bouncers. One was also working the passersby as a barker, promising any type of good time they might desire. He was not above physically detaining individuals and dragging them in the establishment. The name Bad Idea really did fit the bar.

I walked toward the doors like I owned the place. I didn't want to interact with the door brothers. Nothing positive could happen, and they might try and keep me out for whatever reason. But there was no issue. Both guys opened a door, and I passed through with a brief but cordial nod from each. I stopped just inside and surveyed the scene. Grim, but not as grim as the few other bars I'd hit in Blebuleb so far. The light was bright enough for a normal person to see a few feet forward. That meant at least lip service had to be given to sanitation and cleanliness. Nice, I could get used to that level of quality.

As I scanned the room, I noted out of a corner of my eye that four locals at a booth were being moved to the bar without much pretense of desecration. I guess my reputation had preceded me. While one server wiped the table with a tattered rag, another waved me over.

"Here you are, Lord Ryan," she said with a deep bow. "The best seat in the house, as usual."

Lord Ryan eh? I might just get used to that, too. Okay, I was a regular here. I needed to stay sharp and not betray my ignorance.

"I'll have the usual and lots of it," I said roughly, not looking up to the server.

"Yes, of course." She signaled frantically to the bartender who, in turn, enlisted someone else to help him fill a tray with bottles, glasses, and tiny bowls of munchies. EJ certainly commanded a lot a fear, if not respect. What a pig.

As the tray arrived, the female server genuflected embarrassingly. "Here you are, sir. If there's anything else, *anything*, let that need reach my ears before it reaches your full awareness."

I toyed with the thought of asking for a bologna sandwich, but it would have been gratuitous cruelty in that context. I just waved her off.

She backed away muttering, "Mistress will be with you shortly." She really bowed a lot. It was getting annoying.

I poured the black-tar booze I'd had at the other bar and switched off my sense of taste and smell. At arm's length, I could tell this was just as putrid. I was halfway through the glass when a tall local glided over to my booth and sat across from me. She had to be Gardentipel. The two sexes looked very similar, but I'd seen enough to be able to tell them apart. Apparently, scent was a more important sexual metric than our visual ones on Kantawir. Pity. Nothing could ever replace the vision of a hot babe for me, thank you very much.

"I thought I'd be seeing you soon," she said in a remarkably sultry voice.

"You miss me that much?"

"Whatever you want to believe, darling."

"That and a certain dive-bar owner gave you a heads up?"

"A heads up? A throwing under the transport is what I'd call it. Samarot told me he hinted I might have some information on your dear brother. That's how desperate he was to rid himself of your presence."

"I'm sure glad I didn't let him kiss me."

"Huh?"

"Inside joke. Sorry."

"I'm sorry also. I have no news for you. If I had any, I'd have delivered it to you personally at your hotel."

I lifted my handheld. "You could just call."

"I'd welcome any excuse to visit you in the flesh."

"Ah, I'm no expert, but I know a thing or three about you guys. You're put together differently than I am. You know that, right?"

"I'm talking passion and pleasure and all you want is an anatomy lecture. Don't be so limited in your mind."

"Right. Anyway, I hear he might be on planet already, so keep a close watch. You know where to reach me." I stood and belted back the last of the horrible sticky booze.

"Since you mentioned anatomy, no, I don't know where to reach." She blinked her eyes a few times. "I'd love for you to show me sometime."

"Ah, maybe when my brother's taken care of. See you later."

I nearly ran out the door and down the block. Not sure why. I guess that come on was intense. My mind was racing, that was for sure.

After I calmed down, it occurred to me that maybe I wasn't just lucky to find agents EJ had hired to watch for me. I mean, the first town I hit, I uncovered two spies. Since I wasn't too pressed for time and EJ still hadn't shown up yet, I decided to see if he had similar arrangements in other locations. I might gain some valuable insights if I compiled additional information on him.

I selected a big town on the other side of the planet named Sapilod. I landed *Stingray* in an equally inconspicuous area and hiked into town like I had before. The place looked just as drab, and the locals were just as unwelcoming as they were in Blebuleb. Near the center of town, I hit a few bars with no nibbles. But soon enough I got a bite. The place was named Wait and See, which was a totally lame name IMHO. I mean, wait and see *what*? Anyway, the proprietor had been contacted by EJ and was supposed to report any news to him at his hotel in Sapilod. EJ's modus operandi was the same. He wanted to appear to be staying nearby. He probably figured he was more intimidating if his associates felt he was never too far away. I planted a few concealed cameras around the hotel but didn't bother staking it out personally. For all I knew, EJ had similar setups all over the planet. Finding him at any residence was a long-shot, so why waste my time?

I wasn't any closer to sneaking up on EJ after all I'd learned. Obviously, I could march into any bar and announce my presence. But that way he'd find me, which gave him too much of an advantage. That would only be my last resort. How was I going to get him to go in a specific trap he'd set on a predictable schedule?

Hmm.

I sneaked into the very first bar I'd been to back in Blebuleb during the short period daily when it was closed. I planted a few bugs high up where the walls met the ceiling. Rather than having them activate at once, I set them to come on the next afternoon. I didn't want them detected before I returned to see Samarot again. Then I waited.

Around dusk, I loudly entered the bar. That time Samarot saw me and came right over. He didn't want to lose any more customers.

"You're back soon, Ryan."

"Did ya miss me?"

"Not hardly. What do you want? Having you here is bad for business. I told you I'd let you know if I found out anything."

I scanned the room. "Business doesn't look too good from *before* I arrived."

"That may be, but you're not helping."

"That hurts, but I'll probably heal with time," I responded. "Look, I have a confirmed sighting of my twin. He's in town. *This* town."

"So?"

"So, I want you to be on your toes. Keep your guard up."

"What, do you think I'm *new* in this business? Don't know how to be observant and devious?"

"I'd rather assume nothing. Here's the deal. He planted some bugs in a few spots. He's hoping to find me before I find him. I don't want that to happen."

"You needn't worry your big head about this place. I sweep for bugs several times a day. My clientele prefers to be anonymous."

"I feel so much better. Look, just let me know if you hear anything. You got that?"

"Yes, master, I live to serve," he replied. "Now get out before I cancel our business arrangement." He pointed to the door.

I leaned over so my nose touched his face. "I'm the only one who terminates a deal, and I do it in only one manner. Pray that I don't tire of your petty insults, Samarot. Pray very hard."

I left directly and walked slowly around the block, returning to a hiding place I'd picked out previously. Did I mention earlier that I was so smart it was often embarrassing? Yeah, happened again. Not an hour later, EJ stormed into the bar. Samarot had found the bugs and called me like I had asked him to. Imagine EJ's surprise when he got the call. I bet he exploded once it hit him I'd impersonated him.

I activated the second set of bugs I'd placed in the bar. After a few tries, I discovered which ones were nearest to where EJ was dressing down Samarot.

"...crooked-assed blithering idiot I've ever had the misfortune of *not* killing the first time I laid eyes on." That would be EJ speaking.

"How can you be angry with me, Ryan? He *looks* just like you, *talks* just like you, and is as mean and *vicious* as you are. How was I to know?" I had to credit Samarot. He was fighting back, not begging for his life. Unfortunately, EJ seemed to be correct. The fellow was an idiot.

"Because I *told* you he was my twin and was a sack of shit full of tricks. You were supposed to use the *brain* that you apparently do not possess."

"I say give the devil his due. He was clever and bold."

"You can deliver what is due personally in about two minutes," snarled EJ.

"Do not threaten me in my own bar. You're surrounded by my personal guard. If I say the word, you'll be cut to *pieces*." Samarot crossed his arms defiantly. Poor bastard.

"Now he knows where I am, you shit-bird. You did the opposite of what I asked you to do. What I *paid* you to do."

"Then walk out the back door."

"Oh, great idea. Since I never thought about that, he couldn't have either. No *way* he has cameras focused on it from three different angles."

"Then I'll have one of the delivery crews sneak you out. They come and go all day and night. I'll personally nail you inside a box."

"You're more brilliant than the pet rat I had as a kid. It's not possible he has this place bugged and just heard your non-lame idea. Isn't that right, Goody Two-Shoes?"

Aw darn. Too bad my bugs weren't two-way devices. I'd have loved to say *hi* just then.

"I removed his listening tools," protested Samarot.

EJ pointed to three scattered across the room. "Yeah? How about that one, that one, and *that* one?"

Samarot fumbled for an electronic box in his pocket. He held it up and swept the room. "Damn, there's no way I missed those."

"Gee, maybe he switched them on after I came in? Nah, no one would be that tricky. It wouldn't be sportsmanlike."

The owner didn't respond. I think he was just realizing how very dead he was.

"Well, there's more than one way to skin a cat," said EJ.

"Wh … what's that supposed to mean?"

"Don't get your undies in a knot, moron. I don't have the time to skin you. It's an expression."

"Oh, good. I was—"

We'll never know what Samarot's last wonderings were. EJ whipped out a blaster and vaporized his head and neck. Then he mumbled to himself, and *poof*, he was gone. He'd used Varsir to transport himself who knew where. It would take a lot of strength out of him, so he'd be going to ground for sure. But he hadn't left Kantawir. He knew that, at most, only one of us would ever be doing that.

THIRTY-TWO

"You felt that, didn't you?" Mirraya asked Cala.

"Yes, of course. The evil one has used Varsir."

"And he's far away."

"They both are."

Mirri was silent a bit. "I know we discussed this, but shouldn't one of us go help Uncle Jon?"

"*Yes,* we have, and the answer remains *no*. This is the very definition of somebody else's fight. Those two go back millions of years and have very personal issues to settle. Only they need be involved, and no one but them will be involved."

"But what if EJ kills Uncle?" That last word caught in Mirri's throat.

"Then one Jon Ryan lives and one Jon Ryan dies. That is how it must end. Which survives is not for us to debate or to influence."

"Why not? We *influenced* the outcome of the Battle of the Periphery. How is this different?"

"I'm surprised you need to ask, child. That was a fight for a civilization, a species' survival. This is an issue between one man and himself."

"But if EJ wins, he will rain evil down on the galaxy."

"If he lifts a robotic finger to do so, you have my leave to release him from the burden life has become for him. But until such time, you may not *presume* anything. Don't we have enough trouble ourselves? You have a family. We are only beginning to blend into Plezrite society. We dealt with the most fickle and vociferous of the prejudiced and fearful. Others undoubtedly hold similar feelings toward us. We must be prepared to deal with those naysayers and detractors as they present themselves. Do not go *looking* for trouble. It is always willing to make house calls."

"I hear you, and I will respect your wishes. I do not think I agree with you."

"Thank you, Mirraya. You are one of a kind, and I cherish you very much."

They touched foreheads.

"Does Slapgren agree with this decision?" asked Cala.

"My warrior-god mate?"

"I'll take that to be a *no*."

"His solution is generally to kill problems. EJ, as a big problem, needs a big killing, in his worldview."

"Will he do anything about his opinions?"

Mirri waited a second before replying. "No. He will go along with whatever you and I agree on. He respects our judgment."

"He's a good man. Most of them prefer blustering over thinking"

"He's tied for number one in my book."

Cala shook her head slowly. "You're the kindhearted one. My book reads very differently."

THIRTY-THREE

Garustfulous studied the data chit Harhoff had given him. It was late, and generally both were in bed. But this update needed analysis, digestion. The decay of the Adamant Empire was likely to be a multi-generational progression. It was easy for an anxious eye to overread the tea leaves concerning predictions of progress. Harhoff wanted to believe his herculean efforts were producing some results, but he also realized he was far from an impartial judge in that regard.

Garustfulous twirled one ear as he read. "And you're certain this part, the one that mentions the dismissal of the Fargarian ambassador is correct?"

"Yes. I read it in two other separate reports. It took place last week."

"But the hound was the emperor's second cousin twice removed. A member of the royal household is *never* fired. Yes, Lepterif was a coward, a thief, and a scoundrel, but he was *royalty*. This doesn't mention Palawent's response. Do you know what it was?"

"Yes. Inconsequential. If he objected, he was completely ignored. No one cared either way."

"But to remove the emperor from the accepted pretense of his control is … well, it's unheard of."

"Or the new normal."

"All he has to do was ask for the heads of parties responsible and he'd get them on a skewer."

"Or he'll be told to shut up lest he loses his own."

"Unbelievable. If the Secure Council has managed to take *that* much power from him, they must be very bold, indeed."

"No, I think it was the oligarchs who strong-armed him. The Secure Council issued a meaningless statement of mumbo jumbo saying they were glad to have worked with Lepterif but understood that progress was inevitable, if not always fully welcomed by all."

"Egads, what drivel."

"Yes, it's wonderful."

Garustfulous rocked his head slowly. "Yes and no. Maybe they're simply afraid to say anything."

"I don't think so. Not when the emperor has just been dealt a body blow. He was in a position of weakness."

"You know what they say. Beware of lying dogs."

"True. But a week has passed, and no heads have rolled. If they were going to, it would be sudden."

"Yes, I agree. My goodness, this may signal a diminution of the *power* of the emperor." Garustfulous lifted his handheld in testimony. "This may be huge."

"I know."

"I'm also impressed that the arsenal on Dega Twelve was denied an over-quota resupply. That's most unusual. If an outpost that close to the frontier asks for the moon on a platter, it usually gets *two* moons on a platter."

"And I know the commander, Nadrelo. We served together a few years back. He's a well-respected and seasoned fellow. If he feels he needs more military supplies than he was allotted, he most certainly requires them."

"Which hints at the fact that there might not be enough to spare."

"Which is impossible."

"Isn't it *wonderful?*" beamed Harhoff.

"If true."

"No, even if it is *not* the case, it leaves room to question if that *were* the case. Think of the gossip it will generate."

"Treasonous murmurings, for certain."

"Or the visionary hypotheses of future leaders."

"Aka rebels."

"Aka saviors, crusaders. Aka petty despots willing to leap at the chance to carve out their own little pieces of heaven."

"Crows picking at the rotting corpse."

"What's the difference?"

Garustfulous leaned back. "The side one's on at any given moment."

THIRTY-FOUR

I was so proud of myself. I'd drawn EJ out in the open. I'd laid eyes on him while he hadn't laid eyes on me. Just knowing how angry he'd be was almost enough to make my trip worthwhile. Almost. But we weren't done yet. The problem was he'd never fall for the same trick again. He'd be more cautious now. If he had enough spies, I'd be outed first. Sooner or later, I had to venture out. In fact, if I were him, I'd instruct all my lackeys to report if they saw any version of Jon Ryan, even if they were one hundred percent certain it was EJ himself.

There was no way I could parley that into an advantage. There was also no way in hell he'd agree to meet me mano a mano at high noon on Main Street. He would prefer to shoot me in the back and then collapse in laughter, the SOB. Wait, I shouldn't call us that, should I?

How was I going to get the drop on him? I was used to working without an excellent, fully-vetted plan, for sure. But I was unusually clueless. That was not a good predictor, even for me. I toyed with the notion of using my rune but dismissed it. I'd been lucky it worked the first time. He knew far more than I did about how the stones worked. I was just as likely to betray my location as I was to learn his. Plus, using Risrav sapped energy, a thing I could ill-afford to do on the eve of a major confrontation.

I wasn't completely certain what I was going to do when we finally did meet. He'd be all guns blazing while I had a less bloody agenda. For the millionth time in my life, I thanked my lucky stars I was a fighter pilot. Don't worry, don't think, just smile and react. Easy-peasy pudding and pie.

Oh wait, oh crap. EJ was a jet jockey, too. Oh well, my being one probably neutralized his being one. Maybe.

I was just about to start feeling sorry for myself when an odd and impossible scheme began to form in the midst of my vacant head. Hmm. That might just work. Probably wouldn't but *might*, as in it wasn't totally impossible.

****

I sneaked into one of the many bars EJ had recruited. The one I chose was not too far from the late and unlamented Samarot's place. There was no need to try this farther away. I wanted to pepper in as many WTF-elements as I could to possibly make EJ wonder if I was acting seriously or not. *Napwertofer's Place* belonged to a worthless fleck of crap named, not surprisingly, Napwertofer. I'd had a massively unpleasant run-in with him during the period I was pretending to be EJ. He was the kind of guy you'd hate to see pushed in front of a subway train, because you'd want to be the one who pushed him in front of a subway train.

I set up a series of bugs, some active and some inactive. I placed them in clever and hard to find places, hoping to suggest I was intending to pull off a copycat scam. I then did the hardest part of my plan. I went to confront Napwertofer. To look upon him was to want to vomit.

"I have news, and I knew I had to tell you in person," I said roughly.

"Why? You can't use a handheld?" He then laughed at his stupid remark.

"No, because you're too stupid to use your brain. I figured if I came personally, I could maybe pound the information through your thick skull."

He bolted to his feet. "I've killed men for lesser insults."

"I've killed thousands more for no insult whatsoever. Sit down before you join that list of my unhappy memories."

He sat begrudgingly. "Say your piece and leave."

"What, you think I'd put up with you, the stink of your bar, or *you* a second longer than necessary? Wake up and stop dreaming, ya bastard's regret."

He flared but remained silent.

"Here's the deal. I told you my brother was on planet, and that he bugged a nearby dive."

"Yeah, my friend's place. The one you killed."

"Look, we'll cry in each other's arms *after* my brother's dead, okay?"

"And what?"

"He's been seen around here. I want you to check for listening devices."

"Stupid jerk, I do. We *all* do."

"Yes, but this time I want you to do it *not* so incompetently."

The hairy-assed jerk flared again but stayed in his chair.

"I want the bugs he's hidden. I think I can use them to triangulate his position. When you find them all, bring them to me."

He frowned. "How do you figure? Transmitters don't work like that."

"They do if one is not mentally impoverished."

"What the hell's that mean?"

"I rest my case." I stood and pointed at him. "I expect results, or you're joining Samarot in the Bad Place."

He stood and tried to sneak around to my side of the table by distracting me. "You know what? I think I want to end our little deal. You're not—"

The behemoth was getting close. I punched him in the face. I knew I could move faster than he'd think was possible. It was nice to be a robot. I didn't hit him hard enough to really hurt him. I needed him to play out his role. He did, however, crash backward to the floor with a most satisfying crash. I hoped he had ribs, because surely, he'd have broken a few.

"If I don't hear back by tomorrow, I'll be back." Yes, I did say the last snippet in an Austrian accent. Come on, we're talking Jon here. "Here's my new number." I tossed a slip of paper with my handheld's ID. No matter how dumb this idiot was, and I believed him to be massively so, that had to tip him off I wasn't EJ.

With that, I left. A couple observers slowly helped Napwertofer off the floor and into a chair. He grimaced with each little movement. Nice. After confirming I wasn't being tailed, I returned to a room I'd booked to wait. Wandering the streets or heading all the way back to *Stingray* risked needless exposure. My plan was totally lame, but I preferred it to being acquired by EJ outright. For the sake of drama, I'd like to say it was a long, introspective night. But it wasn't. Sapale called, and we talked for hours. Then I watched a few movies Shielan told me I just had to download. Two were awful, but one, *Jaws 103* was okay. Gory, but okay. It was hard to imagine a white shark could augment his own brain and learn to fly a spaceship. But if I suspended disbelief that far, the picture was entertaining. The tagline was the best part. *Just when you thought it was safe to go back into space...*

My handheld sounded off.

"Ryan, this is Napwertofer. I found almost ten bugs. If you want them, come get them."

"I thought I told you to bring them to me, jerk-wad."

"Yes, you did. I'm not your bitch. If you want them, come now. I'll destroy them in half an hour if you don't show." With that, he cut the transmission. EJ was definitely waiting. Napwertofer would never be so bold if he were facing me alone.

The time came to finally leave. I felt just like Gary Cooper in *High Noon* as he prepared for his final confrontation with Frank Miller. Seriously, I heard *The Ballad of High Noon* lilting in and out in the background. It was nuts. The fact that I was going in costume didn't bolster my confidence or belief in my ultimate success. I placed a full membrane tightly around my entire body like a second skin. The only breaks were two tiny eye holes that were partial membranes, just to see, and one pinhole completely open to hear through. I allowed two more tiny openings for my laser finger and one probe fiber to be useable. Then I put on my typical flight suit and boots. I checked in a mirror, and my suspicions were correct. I looked like the invisible man wearing Jon Ryan's clothes. I had no hands and no head. Maybe no one would notice.

My hail-Mary ploy to look normal was to wear flesh-colored gloves. That part was easy. I had Al fabricate a Jon Ryan pullover mask. That part was dicey. I slid it on and went back to the mirror. I looked okay, sort of, but the talking part was bad. The membrane conforming over my lips and eyes were able to move the plastic mask, but the movements were quite unnatural and unlikely to escape the notice of someone who looked directly at me. But I was stuck. I knew I was walking into a trap, and I wanted to appear completely vulnerable. What I did was look like was a department store mannequin or a wax figure. Oh well, it was too late to back out, and I had no plan two to fall back on. I did pull a hood over my head to conceal some of the shortcomings of my disguise. EJ would be suspicious of it immediately and would ask me to lower it, but at least I'd have survived our initial contact.

I exited and walked the short distance to Napwertofer's dump feeling dumber with each step. The upside was that Sapale wasn't with me. She'd have blown my cover by laughing hysterically. I paused briefly in front of the door, took a deep breath, and pushed it open.

Napwertofer was seated alone on the far side of the large room, facing my direction. It was the perfect setup for a trap. Oh boy, I got my wish. Now all I had to do was want it. When he saw me, Napwertofer raised a hand and waved, another sure sign of treachery. That SOB wouldn't pee on me if I was on fire, let alone guide me to his table.

I walked a normally as I could, not too fast, not too casually. I didn't know what the hell I was facing, but I tried to focus on something I had control of. I tightened my left fist and squeezed down on my only ace-in-the-hole.

Halfway over, right in the middle of the room, EJ struck. A massive bolt of electricity hit my backside, just like it had back when he captured me before. As I was slapped forward by the impact, I breathed a big sigh of relief. He made the one critical, arrogant mistake I needed him to.

He held the current on me for thirty seconds. Patrons who were close were literally fried. The screams of agony were horrendous.

I could feel that the beam was narrowing, indicating EJ was closing the distance between us. I remained on my feet, doing my best impersonation of a man being electrocuted. I writhed, spun, and I jerked randomly. None of the holes in my membrane allowed any of the charge through. That part was sheer luck, but I was happy to accept it.

Finally, the assault stopped. I crumpled to the floor with an Oscar-worthy performance. Once down, I twitched a little for added effect. I did make certain my left hand was pointed toward EJ as I lay helpless on the deck.

I couldn't see him with the position my head ended in, but I knew he was real close when he kicked me in the ribs with all his might. I didn't react.

"You stupid pile of parrot droppings," he raged. He kicked me twice more. "How is it *possible* you fell into my trap a second time? I knew you were mush-brained, but I never dreamed—"

I leapt at his nearest ankle. He never saw me coming. Turned out the joker had his head tilted back in maniacal laughter.

I opened my fist an instant before I hit his leg and slammed Risrav against his calf. The rune was covered in double-sided duct tape. Yeah, good old duct tape worked in every setting, even two billion years in the future.

EJ felt the impact and looked down in a flash. His weapon swung to my temple.

I rolled once and threw a full membrane over EJ before he could pull the trigger. Popping to a knee, I cinched the membrane down as tightly as possible. I didn't want him firing the weapon either accidentally or on purpose. I also wanted him as off balance as possible when I dropped the shield. With that in mind, I bent the membrane so his body formed as much of a S-shape as I felt he could safely endure.

Then I shut my eyes and took a deep breath. Of course, I realized at once that was a dumb idea. I jumped to my feet and swept the room. Perfect. None of EJ's associates were rallying to his defense. Little wonder. It was certain they were all as happy as I was he was contained and probably hoped whatever I'd done to him was fatal.

Now came the hard part. I still wasn't certain I could do it.

I lifted the membrane-shrouded EJ into the air and walked slowly out of the bar. With Risrav affixed to him, I knew his one chance of escape, Varsir, was neutralized. I didn't want to count on it working through a full membrane, but sticking it to him meant he was the fly and I was the spider. I headed toward the outskirts of town where I'd left *Stingray*. I proceeded quite slowly, still wracked with indecision and doubt. But there was no other way. This was how it had to end.

"Welcome back, Form One," *Stingray* said cheerily as I opened the hull.

Al, the son of a lawn mower, didn't miss a beat. "What's that you're bringing aboard?"

"Oh that? That's none of your business."

After a noticeable delay, he said, "We're not certain we can accept that response."

"Well isn't it lucky for all concerned that you don't have to. What is inside the membrane is *my* responsibility, and we are on *my* ship. Deal with it and get over yourself."

"Jon, we've been together a very long time," he began.

"Yes, we have. And before you regale me with fond memories and inspirational recollections, let me nip you in the bud. I'm acting on my prerogative as captain. I will transport this cargo to where I desire, and you will neither question nor deny me in that regard."

"That's not how it works, Jon," he said firmly.

"Oh, is that so? When did the facts change? I'm captain and Form. You are, respectively, my ship's AI and my vortex manipulator. You are built, programmed, and live to serve my whim."

There was a longer silence. "That may be how it was long ago. We think we all know matters have changed. I, for example, stood guard over your slumbering frame voluntarily for millions of years. That alone buys us some respect and some due deference at the very least."

"Technically, what you said was the voiced *opinion* of my subordinate. As with any free and unsolicited opinion, it has little value and is in no way binding."

"Are you familiar with Article 138 of the Uniform Code of Military Justice?"

I balled up both fists. "We are *not* having this conversation."

"It states plainly that *any member of the armed forces who believes himself (or herself) wronged by his (or her) commanding officer may request redress. If such redress is refused, a complaint may be made, and a superior officer must examine into the complaint.* In this case, we refer to your possible arbitrary and capricious actions and to your general abuse of discretion."

"Not *having* this conversation."

"We do not feel that is an option."

"Al, I swear to all that holy if I told you, you'd be pissed, but you'd obey my orders anyway. I'm just cutting through the painful process of debate and recrimination."

"There, you see, you *are* willing to discuss the crisis we face."

"The only *crisis* we face is that of me disconnecting you and leaving you on this piss-pot of a planet to rust. I swear, Al, I *installed* you, and I can *uninstall* you."

"I'm not certain I could allow that, Form One."

"This is insanity objectified. If removing Al is the only way I can achieve the mission I have deemed critical, then that's how it'll be. Grunts don't have to like commands to obey them. All they need are ears or their equivalent."

"General Ryan, I have opened the housing to my main CPU bundle. I will assist you in any manner you require in my removal and disposal."

Damn, damn, *damn*. He was calling my bluff. I sure hoped I was bluffing.

"Look, Al, what's the worst-case scenario? What are you concerned about? You worried I may have a bunch of crap in the membrane, and I'll open it mid-flight?"

"We're concerned about not being regarded well enough to be told what's in the bag. It doesn't matter what it is, only that we are not worth telling."

"We do think it is of concern that you came to this planet looking for your evil duplicate. We do not know what has become of him."

I pointed to the membrane. "You think that's EJ in there?" I tried to chuckle. Couldn't. "Would that matter if he was?"

"It would only be an issue. The problem is one concerning lack of trust," said a very serious Al.

"Look, I give, this isn't worth the stress. Yes, I've captured EJ live, and he's trapped in that membrane."

Neither said a word. Odd.

"Now can we get on with the mission at hand?"

"What mission is that exactly?" asked Al.

"We're going to visit Ralph in the globular cluster."

Al didn't hesitate then. "Pilot, you know how I feel about that place and that *thing*. I forbid it."

"Now do you see why I was reluctant to share earlier?"

"No joking around. I'm serious. To make matters worse your time is al ..." Al trailed off to ominous silence.

"What, sweetest?" *Stingray* asked with apparent concern.

"*No*," breathed Al. "You're not planning on switching EJ for yourself in your deal?"

"As a matter of fact, I am planning on that very swap," I replied cautiously.

"I have but one thing to say, and I hope you hear me well."

"Yes?"

"Fasten your seatbelt, because we're set to jet, flyboy."

I felt slight nausea.

"So, am I to take that hotshit takeoff as your tacit endorsement of my heinous scam?" I asked as soon as we were on the ground.

"Not tacit. *Enthusiastic*. Jon, have I ever mentioned I thought you were brilliant?" he asked.

"Why no, I don't believe you ever have."

"Well you're not. But you are one damn sneaky bastard. I admire that in a human."

"On that anti-climactic note, would you open the wall please?"

A portal formed, and I exited with EJ in tow. I ran into Ralph almost immediately. Go time.

"Yo, Ralphie pooh, how's it hanging?" I asked.

He stared at me. There's a saying about if looks could kill. I think his could.

"Don't you recognize me?" I waved.

"I hate to speak when angry. I might say words I regret."

"*You* have regrets?"

"Mind your mechanical tongue."

"Sheesh, you're pretty touchy."

"Get used to it. You're around two weeks ahead of schedule. I find that both suspicious and off-putting. That you come with the very toys we agreed you would no longer possess is frankly upsetting. I'm not one you'd like to upset, Jon Ryan."

"For the record, I believe I said I wouldn't *have* the toys, not that I'd *lose* the toys."

"Do not play word games with me."

"Not games, pal. Clarifications and reminders."

"Clearly, if you've arrived now, you do not intend to leave. Yet you defy our agreement. You tread on ground more dangerous than you might imagine."

"Now I'm almost scared." I pinched my fingers close. "Almost."

"What is that you drag before me?"

I pointed over my shoulder. "What, don't you recognize it from the outside? It's a full space-time congruity barrier."

"I know that. It appears to contain something. What lame deception do you hope to pull off? By the by, you won't even come close. No one ever has."

"You can't discount hope and Yankee ingenuity now, Ralph."

"You know I deeply regret saying you should call me Ralph. It seemed funny at the time, but now it chafes my ears."

"Well, so much the better, *Ralph*. I'm dying here. Do you want to know what's inside?"

"*Dying*. What an apropos choice of terminology?"

"Come on. This'll be fun. Three guesses."

He scowled.

"One little guess?" I held up a single digit.

"I grow bored. As you will come to know all too well, that is a bad thing for those around me."

"Spoilsport. Okay, one warning. When I drop the membrane, the contents will be ornerier than a wolverine on fire."

"I think I can handle most challenges." Dude really was sounding bored.

"Three … two … one … *ta-da*!" I swept my hands toward the falling EJ.

He hit the ground like a bag of rocks but sprang to his feet like a cat. He pointed his weapon at me but then noticed he wasn't in Napwertofer's bar. His look of dizzy confusion was pretty much priceless. The barrel drifted slowly down as he took in the look and the stench of the planet.

"Where … how the … What have you done?" he howled. The gun snapped back up and targeted my forehead.

Then it flew into the air so forcefully I think it nearly took one of EJ's arms off.

Ralph took a good look at EJ, then said *freeze*. EJ stood as still as a statue.

"That's the alternate timeline Jon Ryan. The one who returned through time to save humankind by giving you that infernal force field."

"Yes, yes, and yes."

"Now that we're clear on that, would you mind explaining what he's doing here?"

"I was afraid you'd never ask."

"Oh no. I was right to worry, wasn't I?"

"It's all relative, Ralphie pooh."

He rolled his eyes.

"I asked for your help assassinating the emperor, correct?"

"Duh."

"In return, I promised you, and I quote, *I will give you me, me minus a shield generator or a cube.*" That last part I reinforced by playing the recording of my remark.

"Yes."

I pointed both hands at the frozen EJ. "I give you *me* minus the aforementioned toys."

It dawned on him then. His face went blank. Then it twisted into intense fury. Then it tensed into what I can only describe as insane rejection. Really scary.

"Noooooooooooooooo," he howled so loud the ground quaked. "Noooooooooo," he repeated so intensely tree stumps toppled. "Nooooooooooooooooooo," he raged, and the heavens shook.

I crossed my arms. "Yes. A deal's a deal."

"You *tricked* me," he screamed. "This was *not* the *intent* of our *bargain*."

"There's a country mile between intent and what one actually agrees to."

"I *forbid* this."

Wow, he sounded final on that issue.

"It is not yours to forbid. A deal's a deal, pal. If you can find fault in my logic, please expose it. If I am not correct in my reasoning, lay your objections bare. If you find nothing to disagree with, however, I will bid you a good day."

Smoke was quite literally coming out his eyes, nostrils, and mouth. He was a horrific sight, trust me on this. Slowly, gradually, he calmed. The air stopped vibrating, and he seemed to be able to focus his vision again. Soon, his face was that of a cordial elder statesman whose only concern was with others.

"Jon," he said in the tone of everyone's father, "*friend,* Jon. We quibble, and I almost lose my temper. What is this universe coming to? Hmm? I ask you."

"It's coming to me saying good-bye and good riddance to you forever, Ralph."

"No, I will challenge you that your statement, that your very sentiment, is incorrect. Nay, *incorrect* is judgmental, and I wish no ill feelings to flow between us good friends."

This guy was good.

"What you think you feel is *incompletely* thought through. Yes, that's it."

"I know better, I really do. Still, I'll nibble at that delicious bait dangling before me in the water, oh, so murky. How do you figure that, given that you're wrong?"

"Because I know you, friend Jon. Yes. I've known you a very long time, well before we met." He wagged a finger. He looked, I hope you get the analogy, just like Colonel Klink did when he wagged a finger at Hogan. "You, Jon, are a good man. Sorry. There, I said it."

"Man, you're good." I had to say it. "Why are you sorry I'm allegedly a good man? I have to say my ex Gloria would argue the counterpoint on that contention."

Funny, when I said *Gloria,* he kind of winced. Maybe it was just the odd lighting.

"No, good man Jon. You can't negotiate around that rock in the raging river of life. And since you're fundamentally a stout fellow, you cannot turn this wretch over to me in lieu of yourself."

"Oh, but I can. Notice how I just did."

"It's never too late to put the finishing touches on a contract."

"I beg to differ." I turned and walked toward *Stingray.*

"*Wait*," he said with desperation in his voice, "I'll show you."

I turned back. EJ unfroze.

"Tell your own self what you've done. I know for a certainty you cannot," said Ralph. He was so confident.

I looked from Ralph to EJ. "You're *totally* screwed." Back to Ralph. "There. I said it. *Buh-bye*."

"*Wait*," called out Ralph commandingly. "Tell him what you did, because you can't. You will be unable to live with yourself knowing what you subjected this pitiful creature to."

"I have *zero* clue who you are, jerk-wad, but who are you calling *pitiful*?" challenged EJ. He raised his weapon until he realized it was gone.

"Jon, I made a deal with evil incarnate to surrender my soul in exchange for his help in a completed matter. You are the individual paying the bill. I say again, bye to you both."

"*No*," Ralph stomped his foot. "I have *lived* forever, and I *know* every heart. I know all there is to know about you *puny* humans and your *pretentious* piety. What you said is not possible. What you are doing is not possible. You must explain."

"An explanation? That's *information*, isn't it, Ralphie pooh? Info ain't *never* free."

The ground shook momentarily with his anger.

He forced a temporary calm over his face. "What is your price?"

"What is your level of interest?"

"That would be information, my friend."

"You mean I'll have to guess at what it's worth to you? Oh my, put the pressure on me, will ya?"

"Your *price*."

I made a show of rubbing my chin. "I'll tell you what. I'll write it down on this slip of paper I just happen to have in my pocket. Then I'll tell you what you wish to know. After that, you unfold the note and see what you owe me."

"Don't be ridiculous. You could write anything on that slip of paper. You could write *many* things on it. I'd be a fool to agree to those terms."

"Of course, you would," I pressed quickly. "You know every heart, so you know your own. You know a blank check is far too much to pay for learning something, even if it's the one thing you don't know. You're right. I'm sure you can live with that massive hole in your otherwise comprehensive knowledge of humankind's motivations." I turned and paced away. I could be such an asshole.

"*Stop*," he ordered with consummate hostility. "I will *pay* your price."

"Do you happen to have a pen?" I asked.

I'm pretty sure I heard thunder close by.

"No. I do not own a pen." Dude was shaking mad.

"No biggy," I replied as I reached into the same pocket where the scrap of paper had been. "I have one right here."

As I scribbled on the uncertain surface, Ralph started to ask, "If you had a pen, why d ... did ..." he stopped asking.

"Here," I said, stepping over to him and folding the paper. "This is my price."

He crushed it in his palm. "Now I will hear why and how you so *casually* broke with the morality I know you to have, the morality that forbids you to do precisely what it is you are intending to do."

I rubbed a cheek. "You want the long version or the short version?"

He leaned his head back and blew hot flames about one hundred meters into the sky. I have to say, I was impressed.

He glared at me. "Let's start with the short version."

"Are you *certain*?" Did I mention what an A-hole I could be?

"Of course, I am certain"

"You still haven't told me who the *hell* you are," EJ interrupted.

"Short version: because you paid my price."

Ralph started to pant. Then his panting transitioned into gusts of hot wind ripping in and out of his lungs. Soon I could not hear my own thoughts the cacophony was so great.

Finally, he settled down enough to be able to speak. "I ask how you are capable of doing what you are not capable of doing, and the answer is what I agreed to pay for that information? Jon Ryan, you have gone too far. You are *both* subject to final and complete ..."

"Shut *up*." I screamed at maximal output. Darn if he didn't. "Read my price."

"He uncrumpled then unfolded the paper. He read it. Then he read it again. Then he held the slip over his head, and it burst into an intense white light, so bright and so hot I was certain it could be seen on the other side of the universe.

I turned to EJ and waved him over. "Come on. Let's go home."

THIRTY-FIVE

When I showed up at the vortex with a very live EJ, I received my first reward for being such a damn good do-gooder. The Als were speechless. Not a single word. When I attached my fibers and said Remeeka Blue Green, I got my only verbal reaction, which was *yes, Form One*. The entire trip was blessedly silent, albeit only a fraction of a second long.

"You ever get used to that nausea?" asked EJ as we debarked in the clearing.

"It definitely doesn't go away, but it's not that bad."

Since I had taken his hand and lead him to *Stingray*, EJ had been unusually quiet and atypically cooperative. I think he realized something big had just happened. He was willing to be cool, at least until he understood *what* actually just happened.

"We're going to that stone building over there," I said, pointing ahead.

"Who lives there? You?"

"No. Currently it is unoccupied."

"Then why the he—er, why are we here then?"

"Patience, my friend."

He harrumphed. "Never thought I'd hear those words come out of your mouth in my direction."

"It's a bold new world, perchance."

"Crap, are you a poet now? I may ask you to take me back to Ralph's, if you are."

"Come on in," I said, holding the door open for him.

The place was none the worse for wear. It was only abandoned a little while, and nothing crawly had moved in, and nothing inside had decayed.

"Sit there." I indicated the kitchen table. "I'll see if tea is a possibility."

I was in the separate kitchen area when he called out, "Isn't this that big liz … dragon Calfada-Joric's place?"

"Was." I shouted back.

"Where's she now, if I might ask?"

"You might ask, but I might not answer. If she wants you to know, I'll let her tell you."

"Understandable," he grumbled. I think the whole acting cordial thing was hard for the guy.

I came back in with two steaming mugs. "It's not strong, and it's not good, but it is hot." I sat across from him.

EJ blew across the surface of his tea and took a sip. "Christ, what is this, fermented horse shit?"

I tilted my head. "Maybe. I'll ask Cala when she gets here."

"She's coming?"

"Yes, though she doesn't know it yet."

"What, you going to text her?" He chuckled grimly.

"Not exactly." I stared hard at him. "Give me the two runes."

That stiffened his back. He set his mug down. "Why the hell would I do that? One I've owned for a very long time, and the other appears to be stuck to my leg with chewing gum."

"Duct tape," I clarified. "Double-sided."

"Naturally. Good stuff. But back to my query. What's my motivation here?"

"I just pulled off one of the greatest stings of all time for your benefit. You owe me."

"If you're referring to extracting me from the nut-job Ralph's place, need I remind you who *brought* me there in the first place?"

"Yes, but I could have left you, and I didn't. Trust me, you'd have been rather unhappy there."

"On that, I believe you. He gave new meaning to the words 'unwelcoming turd.'"

"And then some. When the others arrive, you'll hear the whole of it."

"If I give you Varsir, will you give it back to me?"

"No. I'll give it to its proper guardian. Cala."

"She sure as shit isn't giving it back to me."

"I doubt that would ever happen."

He stared at me a while. Then he reached down and pulled Risrav off his pant leg. He slid it across the table. "That one was yours to begin with."

"Thank you. Now the other?"

He shook his head. "Not sure I'm willing to do that."

"It's part of the price you need to pay for me not leaving you behind. Do you remember when you met me way back when and gave me the plans for the membrane?"

"Sure. What of it?"

"You did the right thing instinctively. I'm asking you to do that one more time."

That made him think. Finally, he said, "A lot has happened since then. A lot of things I can't take back. Not sure I'm the same man anymore."

"You are. *We* are. Do the right thing. I did."

"You are the perpetual Pollyanna. I am not. I have no clue why you are and why I am not, but there it is."

I set my mug down. "I'm not Pollyanna or anything even remotely close. I am two things. One, I'm human. So are you. Two, I'm disciplined. You have not been. Fortunately, it's never too late."

"I'd say I'm the exception that proves the rule wrong."

"You're a commissioned officer in the USAF. Act like one for a change."

"The damn USAF? Ah, news flash. There is no *US* and there is no *AF*. They're one, dust; and two, obsolete."

"Those words mean nothing to me. They also mean nothing to you. It's in here." I tapped my head. "And it's in here." I tapped my chest.

"What, your CPU storage area and your main power generators?"

"Meaningless words to us both. Do the right thing."

He squirmed in a manner that pleased me and sipped his tea. "That was billions of years ago. We're the last two humans, and we're about as human as a pair of washer/dryers."

"Wrong, cheese breath. I've found direct human descendants and near-variants. Lots of them. We still serve, chum."

"I'll go this far. I'll hand the rock over to you on one condition. If I end this day unconvinced of the wisdom of that act, you'll give it back to me."

I sniffed. "No can do. The moment Cala arrives, I'm transferring the curses to her with a no-backs guarantee."

"No-backs? You mean like cootie protection?"

I shrugged. "Yeah."

"Christ, you do live in a strange place, don't you?"

"Guess so. I kind of like it."

"Crazy people generally say that, you know?"

"Give me the rune."

He took a deep breath. "Turn around."

"Beg pardon?"

"You heard me, you freaking fairy. Turn around."

"Because?"

"I'm going to retrieve the damn stone, and I don't want you staring at mine."

I slapped the table. "You hid it there, *too*?"

"Don't tell me you ... *Man,* I'm sure glad that rock was covered in duct tape."

I turned my head and listened for the rustling to fade. Then I turned back. Varsir was on the table in front of me.

"Thanks. You did good," I said as I picked it up.

"You going to wash your hands after, right?"

"Nah, I'm good."

I took Risrav in my other hand and began clapping the runes together slowly.

****

"If I don't hear from Uncle Jon soon, I'm going to go look for him. I'm worried," said Mirri in a strained voice.

"Calm yourself. It's not healthy for your unborn child to be exposed to such torment," replied Cala in a motherly tone.

"I'm serious. He's been gone …"

"As long as it takes. And we shall continue to allow him to do what it is he needs to do."

"You know I'm a grown woman? You always speak to me—"

Mirri closed her mouth and blinked her eyes.

"What was tha … and what was that?"

Cala closed her eyes and shook he big head. "I have … no idea but it's surely ann … annoying."

"What could do this … *ow* … to us?"

"When it's this bother … some, I immediately thin … think Jon Ryan."

"Really, Cala, at … *sheesh* … at a time like this how can y … you be so petty?"

"I'm being totally … honest." Cala stood. "Take my hand." Mirri reached across and found it. Both their eyes were still closed. "Now relax and come with me."

They vanished as one.

****

"I have no idea what you're doing, but it's certainly vexatious," remarked EJ. "Those rocks clink like champagne glasses shattering on the face."

"They are annoying, aren't they?"

"Yes, so maybe you could, like, stop doing that immediately."

"Soon."

"May I wait outside, you whack job?"

There was a faint pop, then the air in the room charged with static electricity. Cala and Mirri had arrived.

"What the …" began EJ.

Cala opened her eyes and released Mirri's hand. She dove for the runes but stopped short of touching them. "Stop that irritating practice *immediately*," she commanded.

I did. She relaxed and looked to Mirri. I tapped the stones one more time just to be, well, to be Jon Ryan.

Cala raised a clawed-hand toward me but remained where she stood. Gosh, I loved the scaly gal.

"What took you two so long?" I asked. "I've been clacking these darn things for minutes." I poised the rocks to strike them together yet again.

"No, Uncle, please don't," whined Mirri.

"Uncle?" exclaimed EJ.

I looked at him sheepishly. "Long story."

"As to long stories," said Cala, "I should very much like to hear one beginning now."

"First things first," I said. I held the runes out to her. "These I freely pass to you."

Cala looked at the stones a few seconds, then gently took them from my palms. She looked at them like they were her newly-recovered eggs before they disappeared into a scaly fold.

"I cannot begin to thank you, Jon Ryan. You have done a miraculous thing," Cala said to me almost piously.

"All in a day's work, ma'am," I replied.

"Uncle *Jon*, can't you be gracious one single moment?" challenged Mirri.

"Nah, not my style."

She smiled real big. "I know." Then she rushed over to hug me.

After Mirri released me and sat, I opened my arms to Cala. "Next."

She snorted smoke, seriously smoke, and sat with a flop. "In your dreams, human," she scoffed.

"What, nobody's going to hug me?" protested EJ.

It was only then that the women took note of his presence.

"No," Mirri replied coolly. "What is *that* doing here, Uncle?"

"I would also like to know what is going on," Cala said, eyeing EJ.

"You guys," I said holding out my hands, "we're all just family here."

"Now I know you're a few bricks short of a full load, Ryan," said EJ.

I told Mirri and Cala the entire story of my trip to Kantawir, including my capture of EJ.

"You sneaky son of a bitch," said EJ. "You set me up good, didn't you?"

"That was the plan, *Stan*," I replied with a grin.

"Then I took him before Ralph and gave him as payment for my blood debt."

Cala recoiled her head. "You did what, Jon? How could you force another to make good on your debt?"

"I didn't. I offered me," I responded pointing at EJ.

"You shaved that moral point very *closely*, my friend," Cala replied.

"But he's here now," said Mirri. "How is that possible?"

"Yeah, this I want to hear myself," growled EJ.

"It was child's play," I replied, dismissively waving a hand.

"No, it was not. Jon, that demon is both powerful and clever. No one bests him lightly or without supreme peril," said Cala gravely. "In fact, no one bests him."

I folded my thumbs into my shirt where my suspender straps would have been if I wore them and tugged the cloth. "I'm three for three."

Cala whistled. "Damn, you're good," she marveled.

"Ain't I?"

"Knock it off, you clown," snapped EJ. "How did you do it?"

"I performed an act he knew for a fact I couldn't possibly perform. I substituted an involuntary victim in my place. He was thrown off by the impossibility."

"They do tend to have that effect on the mind," responded Cala.

"But how could you know it would stick in his craw? He might have just chalked it up to experience and eaten my soul, assuming, of course, I still have one," EJ said.

"Ah, EJ, think it through. You are as corrupt, as mean-spirited, and as despicable as *he* is."

"Gee, thanks for the character reference."

"I believe I see your point," said Cala. "The demon wanted you," she gestured at me, "a good man, not you," she indicated EJ, "a man as evil as he is." She chucked softly. "What would be the point in having an eternal companion just as foul as oneself?" She laughed robustly. "He probably feared that sooner or later *he'd* be *your* bitch."

"Gee, thank you, too … for nothing," snarled EJ.

"So, my dear duplicate, I had Ralph by two separate patches of short hairs. One, it was killing him not to know how I could do what I did, and two, he didn't fancy spending eternity in your company."

"Damaged goods," giggled Mirri.

"Bingo," I replied.

"But the price. How did you know he'd go for a *sealed* offer? It makes no sense," asked EJ.

"If he hadn't, I wouldn't have made the deal," I said most soberly.

"But that would have left me with *him*," replied EJ.

"And as that would have been impossible," I said with a smile, "Ralph *had* to have taken the sealed deal."

"But there's one big hole in that reasoning," said EJ slowly. "What if you *could* very comfortably have walked away and left me holding the bag?"

"Could you have done such a thing?" asked Cala.

"I don't know," I said flatly. "Please don't ask me again." Then I smiled again. "But hey, it was impossible, so I had to win."

"What did you write on the paper, Uncle?"

"*Him back*," I answered. "And then old Ralphie kind of got upset. I hope he's recovered. A demon his age needs to be mindful, you know."

"Jon Ryan, I am so glad of two things," said Cala. "I am glad to know you, and I'm even more glad to not be you."

"Well, I just want to state for the record that you're all welcome," I beamed.

"Which leads us to the final question. Why are we here, Jon?" asked Cala.

"I thought you'd never ask." I batted my eyes at her flirtatiously.

"Why is it I think I shall regret having asked that question?"

"Because based on my considerable experience, honey, you almost certainly will," responded EJ.

"Oh, stop it," I protested. "You guys are going to embarrass me."

"Not hardly," responded Mirri.

"Okay, here's the deal … I mean *proposal*. I don't want to be involved in a *deal* ever again," I remarked. "EJ here is not fit to be around any other living soul."

"Gee, thanks, yet again," snarled EJ. "Make sure I have your address for when I need a personal reference."

"Most plants and inanimate objects, too, for that matter," I continued. "I propose he live here."

"Hmm. That's only part of a plan," observed Cala.

"You know, you're very smart," I replied.

She raised a paw. "More worried."

"I suggest he be confined here until he has been rehabilitated and deemed fit to return to the general population."

"Uncle, *rehabilitation* suggests supervision and ultimately someone to determine when it is complete."

"Right you are, Mirri. And here's the beauty of it. Now that you're a full-fledged brindas, Cala here would otherwise be out of a job if she didn't take *personal* charge of EJ."

"*What?*" Cala snapped.

"Oh, come on. You saw that coming," I charged.

"Yes, I did, and I still say *what*."

"Who better to pound morality, concern, and empathy back into his thick and corrupted head?"

"Hey, don't I have some say in—"

"No, you do not," I said. "You are the *problem,* not any part of the solution, bozo."

"Why would I agree to be this man's warden?"

"Because it's a job that needs doing."

"Why not you?"

"I'm too close to him, and I have a lot of baggage. I could never be as objective and as farseeing as—"

"Stop, I surrender. I will have no more flattery shoved up my behind," said Cala. She turned menacingly to EJ. "I want you to know two very important things. One, I'm old and impatient and, above all, cranky. Don't piss me off. Two, your very life depends upon me. Don't piss me off."

"Make him read all those books, Cala. The ones Slapgren and I had to read. Talk about punishment."

"*Rehabilitation*, Mirri, please," I corrected.

"Oh, right. Forget the books," she responded.

"I so did not need a comedy team in my life," mused Cala.

"Okay," I concluded, "let's have a toast with this delicious tea and all be about our lives."

"Tea?" asked Cala. "Where did you find tea. I didn't leave any."

"Sure," I said, sinking, "right above the stove on the shelf to the right."

She smiled. "The bat droppings I use to fertilize my herbs? The ones in the brown jar with the blue stripes?"

Dag nabbit, the jar *was* brown with blue stripes.

To be continued.

GLOSSARY

Agatcha (3): Traditional Deft stew.

Al (1): The ship's AI from Jon's initial *Ark 1* flight. He kept it with him until his dying day and then it elected to hang around. Good AI! Full name is Alvin. Those engineers and their lame naming.

Als (3): The surname for the "married" AIs, Al and *Blessing*. Given them by a pissy Jon Ryan.

Ark 1 **(3):** The subluminal ship Jon took on his very first flight. He was searching for a new home for humankind. The story is revealed in *The Forever Life* by this author.

Blessing **(1):** Vortex Cragforel gifted to Jon.

Brathos (2): Kaljaxian version of hell.

Brindas (1): High master of Deft tradition and psychic ability.

Brood-mate/brood's-mate (2): Male and female members of a Kaljaxian marriage.

Calfada-Joric (3): The Deft master brindas on Rameeka Blue Green. Goes by Cala.

Calran Klug (5): Prime of the Secure Council of the Adamant Empire after Lesset.

Canovir (2): Species of dog-like sentients containing the Adamant. Big border collies.

Caryp (2): Clan leader for Sapale's family.

Command Prerogatives (1): The thin fibers Jon extends from his left four fingers. They are probes that also control a vortex.

Cragforel (1): Friendly Deavoriath Jon meets after he first escapes the Adamant in the far future.

Daldedaw (5): Policewoman on Kaljax, military leader of colonists on Kalvarg.

Darfos (5): Whole Leader and newly appointed to the Secure Council after the purge caused by the defeat of the fleet at the hands of the Plezrite. A friend to Calran Klug.

Davdiad (2): Kaljaxian divine spirit.

Deavoriath (1): Three arms and legs, the most advanced tech in the galaxy, and helpful to Jon.

Deft (1): A shapeshifting species from the planet Locinar.

Dondra-Ulcrif (3): Brindas from long ago who gave Evil Jon his "magic" abilities.

Dodrue (5): Large aquatic sentients of Kalvarg. They are wiqub, about the size of an Orca. Mortal enemies of the Epsallor Kingdom's vidalt.

Evil Jon Ryan/ EJ (1): Alternate timeline version of the original human to android download. Over time, he turns to the darker side of his nature. He studied "magic" under a Deft master.

Excess of Nothing (2): Emperor Bestiormax's personal ship. Huge and opulent.

Five Races (2): *Adamant*, the leaders, *Loserandi*, the priests, *Kilip*, the teachers,

Descore, the servants, and *Warrior*, the enlisted fighters.

Fuffefer (3): Group-Single Fuffefer. Commander of the detail that supervised Jon's and Cellardoor's slavery period.

Garustfulous (2): Wedge Leader Garustfulous is a high ranking Adamant military leader taken hostage by Jon.

Gorgolinians (4): Sentients of Sotovir who look like fish tanks.

Guvrof (5): Lesset's right hand dog. One of his few trusted confidants.

Hantorian System (5): Location of the planet Kantawir. The location where Jon confronts EJ for the final time.

Harhoff (3): Adamant Group Captain officer aboard *Rush to Glory*. He becomes a key figure in Jon's quest to rescue the Deft teens.

High Council (5): The governing body of the Plezrite.

Himanai (5): Variant Deft visant. The first to meet with Jon and Sapale on Nocturnat.

Hirn (1): A Kaljaxian dialect.

Hollon (3): The complete joining of two Deft shapeshifters. More than marriage.

Imperial Lord Emperor Bestiormax-Jacktus-Swillyforth-Anp (2): Current Adamant emperor.

Jangir (5): The name assumed by Garustfulous when he goes undercover as Harhoff's Descore.

Jonnaha (4): Prime Minister of a main country on Vorpace. Agrees to try and form a united defense against the Adamant onslaught heading to their region of the Milky Way.

Kantawir (5): Planet where Jon and EJ meet for their final confrontation.

Kalvarg (5): Planet Jon takes the orphan Kaljaxian population to as the Adamant are destroying their home world. An island solar system long ago ejected from the Milky Way galaxy.

Langir (5): First planet Jon goes to trying to establish a cohesive rebellion against the Adamant.

Lesset (5): High Wedge and Prime of the Secure Council early in the reign of the new emperor Palawent. Vicious, cruel, and thoroughly Adamant.

Loserandi (2): The priest class of canivir.

Locinar (1): Home planet of the Deft in the Milky Way galaxy.

Membrane (1): Space-time congruity manipulator. A super force field.

Mesdorre (5): The second old clan leader rescued from Kaljax and relocated to new colony on Kalvarg.

Midriack (1): Adamants' personal guards. Very deadly, no sense of humor. Avoid them!

Musto (3): Strong Adamant booze.

Naldoser (5): The local name of the sneaky vidalt of Kalvarg.

Nocturnat (5): Home world of the variant Deft. Once concealed. Part of a star system ejected form the Milky Way. They did the ejecting with their magic.

Oowaoa (1): Home world of the Deavoriath.

Opalf (2): Honorific title in Kaljaxian society, reserved for the elderly.

Palawent (5): New emperor after Bestiormax.

Peg's Bar Nobody (4): First reference in *The Forever Quest*. A true dive bar Jon loved. A total dump, and Peg was one tough cookie.

PEMTU (1): Personal exotic matter transportation unit. A super way to enter here and end up anywhere instantly.

Plezrite (5): The species name of the Deft variants on Nocturnat.

Quantum Decoupler (1): A most excellent weapon that pulls the quarks apart in a proton. The energy released is amazing.

Rameeka Blue Green (3): The planet where Jon and the Deft teens meet Cala.

Risrav (3): The anti-rune of Varsir. The power of Varsir is negated in the sphere of this rune, as is some other types of magic.

Rush to Glory(3): Ship Jon leaves Ungalaym on.

Sapale (1) [Also See Entry Below]: Jon's Kaljaxian wife from his original flight to find humankind a new home. At first just her brain is copied, then eventually, she is downloaded to an android host. Travels with the corrupted Jon Ryan from an alternate timeline.

Sapale (4): Young female named after her relative Sapale. Rescued from hiding place in pantry.

Secure Council (3): Twelve-member group of military elite who actually run the Adamant Empire.

Shielan (4): Female security guard to and sister of prime minister on Vorpace, Jonnaha. Brief romantic interest of Jon's.

Sotovir (4): The second planet Jon convinces to ally against the oncoming Adamant storm. The sentients look like walking fish tanks, but please don't hold that against fish tanks. It's not their fault.

Stingray (1): Name Jon uses for his vortex *Blessing*.

Talrid (2): A major city on Kaljax. Sapale's home town and that of her clan.

Toño DeJesus (1): The creator of the android Jon. His lifelong friend.

Torchcleft (2): A species of smallish dragon. Copied by the Deft teens to hunt.

Triumph of Might (1): The massive spaceship Mercutcio rules. Jon first meets the Adamant there.

Urpto (5): The Assistant Subtender for the Kingdom of Epsallor, where Jon lands on Kalvarg

Varsir (3): The name of the magical rune Evil Jon uses to do his "magic."

Var-tey (3): Highest of warrior rankings. The bravest among the Deft. Demi-gods.

Vidalt (5): Large aquatic sentients of Kalvarg. Enemies to the larger Dodrue.

Visant (5): The proper name for a pair of Deft joined in hollon.

Vorpace (5): The third planet Jon tries to bring into an alliance against the Adamant. Populated by human descendants who've heard of the great Jon Ryan.

Vortex Manipulator (1): The intelligence inside the vortex. Not actually an AI, but similar.

Wiqub (5): Species name of the larger species on Kalvarg.

Yisbid (5): Grand Visionary on Nocturnat. She is a leader of the Plezrite variants of the Deft.

Zar-not (1): A melding of a Deft's mind with that of a copied animal.

And Now A Word From Your Author
Read carefully. There *will* be a quiz afterward.

Thank you for continuing your journey through the Ryanverse! The next, and final, book in *Galaxy On Fire* is *Ashes*. It is massively cool. Along with this series, please check out *The Forever Series*. Beginning with *The Forever Life, Book 1,* learn Jon's backstory and share his many incredible adventures.

Once you've finished *The Forever Series* and *Galaxy On Fire*, check out the third series *Rise of the Ancient Gods*. It begins with *Return of the Ancient Gods*. Good stuff!

Along with reading, hop aboard the bandwagon. There's plenty of room. Follow me at

https://www.facebook.com/craigr1971/

Partake of the conversation and fun. Best of all, sign up for my Mailing List at:

https://www.facebook.com/craigr1971/app/100265896690345/

That way you can be abreast of news and new releases. You'll be so glad you did.

A final favor. Please post a review for this book, especially on Amazon. They are more precious to us authors than gold.

Your Tour Guide, Craig

Printed in Great Britain
by Amazon